The Find-Outers

The Mystery of
the Invisible Thief

Hodder
Children's
Books

HODDER CHILDREN'S BOOKS

First published in Great Britain in 1943
This edition published in 2016 by Hodder and Stoughton

1 3 5 7 9 10 8 6 4 2

Text copyright© Hodder and Stoughton, 1943
Enid Blyton's signature is a Registered Trade Mark of Hodder and Stoughton

A CIP catalogue record for this book is available from the British Library.

ISBN 978 1 444 93084 9

Typeset in Meridien by Avon DataSet Ltd, Bidford-on-Avon, Warwickshire

Printed and bound in Great Britain by Clays Ltd, St Ives plc

The paper and board used in this book are made from
wood from responsible sources.

Hodder Children's Books
An imprint of Hachette Children's Group
Part of Hodder and Stoughton
Carmelite House
50 Victoria Embankment
London EC4Y 0DZ

An Hachette UK Company
www.hachette.co.uk

www.hachettechildrens.co.uk

CONTENTS

1. ONE HOT SUMMER'S DAY

'Do you know,' said Pip, 'this is the fourth week of the summer holidays – the fourth week, mind – and we haven't even *heard* of a mystery!'

'Haven't even smelt one,' agreed Fatty. 'Gosh, this sun is hot. Buster, don't pant so violently – you're making me feel even hotter!'

Buster crawled into a patch of shade, and lay down with a thump. His tongue hung out as he panted. Bets patted him.

'Poor old Buster! It must be terrible to have to wear a fur coat this weather – one you can't even unbutton and have hanging open!'

'Don't suggest such a thing to Buster,' said Fatty. 'He'd look awful.'

'Oh dear – it's too hot even to laugh,' said Daisy, picturing Buster trying to undo his coat to leave it open.

'Here we are – all the Five Find-Outers – and Dog,' said Larry, 'with nothing to find out, nothing to solve, and eight weeks to do it in! Fatty, it's a waste of the hols. Though even if we had a mystery, I think I'd be too hot to think about clues and suspects and what-nots.'

The five children lay on their backs on the grass. The sun poured down on them. They all wore as little as possible, but even so they were hot. Nobody could bear poor Buster being near them for more than two seconds, because he absolutely radiated heat.

'Whose turn is it to fetch the iced lemonade?' said Larry.

'You know full well it's yours,' said Daisy. 'You always ask that question when it's your turn, hoping somebody will get it out of turn. Go and get it, you lazy thing.'

Larry didn't move. Fatty pushed him with his foot. 'Go on,' he said. 'You've made us all feel thirsty now. Go and get it.'

A voice came up the garden. 'Bets! Have you got your sunhat on? And what about Pip?'

Bets answered hastily. 'Yes, Mother – it's quite

all right. I've got mine on.'

Pip was frowning at her to warn her to say nothing about him. He had, as usual, forgotten his hat. But his mother was not to be put off.

'What about Pip? Pip, come and get your sunhat. Do you want sunstroke *again*?'

'Blow!' said Pip, and got up. Larry immediately said what everybody knew he would say.

'Well, you might as well bring back the iced lemonade with you.'

'You're very good at getting out of your turn,' grumbled Pip, going off. 'If I'd been quick enough, I'd have told you to get my hat when you got the lemonade. All right, Mother. I'm COMING!'

The iced lemonade revived everyone at once. For one thing they all had to sit up, which made them feel much more lively. And for another thing, Pip brought them back a bit of news.

'Do you know what Mummy just told me?' he said. 'Inspector Jenks is coming to Peterswood this afternoon!'

'*Is* he?' said everyone, intensely interested. Inspector Jenks was a great friend of theirs. He admired the Five Find-Outers very much, because

3

of the many curious mysteries they had solved. 'What's he coming for?' asked Fatty. 'There's not a mystery on, is there?'

'No, I'm afraid not,' said Pip. 'Apparently his little goddaughter is riding in the gymkhana in Petter's Field this afternoon, and he's promised to come and see her.'

'Oh – what a disappointment,' said Daisy. 'I thought he might be on the track of some exciting case or other.'

'I vote we go and say hello to him,' said Fatty. Everyone agreed at once. They all liked the burly, good-looking Inspector, with his shrewd twinkling eyes and teasing ways. Bets especially liked him. Next to Fatty, she thought he was the cleverest person she knew.

They began to talk of the mysteries they had solved and how Inspector Jenks had always helped them and encouraged them.

'Do you remember the missing necklace and how we found it?' said Larry. 'And that hidden house mystery – that was super!'

'The most exciting one was the mystery of the secret room, *I* think,' said Pip. 'Gosh, I shall never forget how I felt when I climbed that tree by the big empty house – looked into a room at the top and found it all furnished!'

'We've had some fun,' said Fatty. 'I only hope we'll have some more. We've never been so long in any holidays without a mystery to solve. The old brains will get rusty.'

'Yours could never get rusty, Fatty,' said Bets admiringly. 'The things you've thought of! And your disguises! You haven't done any disguising at all these hols. You aren't tired of it, are you?'

'Gosh, no,' said Fatty. 'But for one thing, it's been too hot – and for another, old Mr Goon's been away, and the other policeman in his place is such a stodge. He never looks surprised at anything. I'll be quite glad when Mr Goon comes back and we hear his familiar yell of "You clear orf!" Old Buster'll be pleased too – you miss your ankle hunt, don't you, Buster?'

Bets giggled. 'Oh dear – the times Buster has danced round Mr Goon's ankles and been yelled at. Buster really is wicked with him.'

'Quite right too,' said Fatty. 'I hope Mr Goon comes back soon, then Buster can have a bit of exercise, capering round him.'

Buster looked up at his name and wagged his tail. He was still panting. He moved near to Fatty.

'Keep off, Buster,' said Fatty. 'You scorch us when you come near. I never knew such a hot dog in my life. We ought to fix an electric fan round his neck or something.'

'Don't make jokes,' begged Daisy. 'It's honestly too hot to laugh. I don't even know how I'm going to walk to Petter's Field this afternoon to see the Inspector.'

'We could take our tea and ask the Inspector, plus goddaughter, to share it,' said Fatty.

'Brilliant idea!' said Daisy. 'We could really talk to him then. He might have a bit of news. You never know. After all, if there's any case on, or any mystery in the air, he's the one to know about it first.'

'We'll ask him,' said Fatty. 'Get *away*, Buster. Your tongue is dripping down my neck.'

'What we want, for a bit of excitement,' said Pip, 'is a nice juicy mystery, and Mr Goon to come back and make a mess of it as usual, while we do all the solving.'

'One of these days, Mr Goon will do all the solving and we'll make a mess of it,' said Daisy.

'Oh *no*,' said Bets. 'We couldn't possibly make a mess of it if Fatty's in charge.' The others looked at her in disgust – except Fatty, of course, who looked superior.

'Don't set Fatty off, for goodness' sake,' said Pip. 'You're always hero-worshipping him. He'll be telling us of something wonderful he did last term now.'

'Well, as a matter-of-fact, I forgot to tell you, but something rather extraordinary *did* happen last term,' said Fatty. 'It was like this . . .'

'I don't know the beginning of this story but I'm sure I know the end,' said Larry gloomily.

Fatty was surprised. 'How can you know the end if you don't know the beginning?' he asked.

'Easily, if it's to do with you,' said Larry. 'I'm sure the end will be that you solved the extraordinary happening in two minutes, you caught the culprit, you were cheered and clapped to the echo and you had "As brilliant as ever" on your report. Easy!'

Fatty fell on Larry and soon they were rolling over and over on the grass with Buster joining

7

in excitedly.

'Oh shut up, you two,' said Pip, rolling out of the way. 'It's too hot for that. Let's decide about this afternoon. Are we going to take our tea or not? If we are, I'll have to go and ask my mother now. She doesn't like having it sprung on her at the last minute.'

Larry and Fatty stopped wrestling, and lay panting on their backs, trying to push Buster off.

'Yes, of course we're going to take our tea,' said Fatty. 'I thought we'd decided that. There'll be tea in the marquee in Petter's Field, of course, but it'll be stewing hot in there, and you know what marquee teas are like. We'll take ours and find the Inspector. He won't like marquee teas any more than we do, I'm sure.'

'There's a dog show as well as the gymkhana,' said Bets. 'Couldn't we enter Buster – or is it too late?'

'The only prize he'd win today is for the hottest dog,' said Fatty. 'He'd win that all right. Buster, keep *away* from me. You're like an electric fire.'

'We'd better go,' said Larry, getting up with a groan. 'It takes twice as long to get back home this hot weather – we simply crawl along! Come on,

Daisy, stir yourself!'

Daisy and Larry went down the drive and up the lane to their own home. Pip and Bets didn't have to move because they were already at home! Fatty found his bicycle and put his foot on the pedal.

'Buster!' he called. 'Come on. I'll put you in my bike basket. You'll be a grease-spot if you have to run all the way home.'

Buster came slowly up, his tongue out as usual. He saw the cook's cat in the hedge nearby, but he felt quite unable to chase it. It was just as well, because the cat felt quite unable to run away.

Fatty lifted Buster up and put him in his basket. Buster was quite used to this. He had travelled miles in this way with Fatty and the others.

'You'll have to take some of your fat off, Buster,' said Fatty, as he cycled down the drive. 'You're getting too heavy for words. Next time you see Mr Goon, you won't be able to dance round him, you'll only waddle!'

A call came from Pip's house. 'Lunch,' said Pip sitting up slowly. 'Come on – I hope it's salad and jelly – that's about all I want. Don't let's forget to ask Mummy about a picnic tea for this afternoon.

She'll probably be glad to get rid of us.'

She was! 'That's a good idea!' she said. 'Tell Cook what you want – and if you take drinks, *please* leave some ice in the fridge. You took it all last time. Yes – a picnic is certainly a very good idea – I shall have a lovely peaceful afternoon!'

2. AT THE GYMKHANA

The five children, and Buster of course, met in Petter's Field about three o'clock. The gymkhana had already begun, and horses were dashing about all over the place. Buster kept close to Fatty. He didn't mind passing the time of day with one or two horses in a field, but thirty or forty galloping about were too much.

'Anyone seen the Inspector?' asked Daisy, coming up with a big basket of food and drink.

'No, not yet,' said Fatty, getting out of the way of a colossal horse ridden by a very small boy. 'Is there any place in this field where there aren't horses tearing about? Buster will have a heart attack soon.'

'Look over there,' said Bets, with a giggle. 'See the woman who's in charge of that hoopla stall, or whatever it is? She might be Fatty dressed up!'

They all looked. They saw what Bets meant at once. The woman had on a big hat with all kinds of flowers round it, a voluminous skirt, very large feet, and a silk shawl pinned round her shoulders.

'Fatty could disguise himself like that beautifully!' said Daisy. 'Is she real – or somebody in disguise?'

'Inspector Jenks in disguise!' said Bets, with a giggle, and then jumped as somebody touched her on the shoulder.

'What's that you're saying about me?' said a familiar voice. All five of them swung round at once, their faces one big smile. They knew that voice!

'Inspector Jenks!' said Bets, and swung on his broad arm. 'We knew you were coming!'

'Good afternoon, sir,' said Fatty, beaming. 'I say, before anyone else gets hold of you – would you care to have a picnic tea with us – and bring your goddaughter too, of course? We've brought plenty of food.'

'So it seems,' said Inspector Jenks, looking at the three big baskets. 'Well, I wondered if I would see you here. Yes, I'd love to have tea with you – and so would Hilary – that's my small goddaughter. Well, Find-Outers – any more mysteries to report?

What exactly are you working on now?'

Fatty grinned. 'Nothing, sir. Not a mystery to be seen or heard in Peterswood just now. Four weeks of the hols gone and nothing to show. Awful waste of time.'

'And Goon is away, isn't he?' said the Inspector. 'So you can't bait him either – life must indeed be dull for you. You wait till he comes back though – he'll be full of beans. He's been taking some kind of refresher course, I believe.'

'What's a refresher course?' asked Bets.

'Oh – improving his police knowledge, refreshing his memory, learning a few new dodges,' said the Inspector. 'He'll be a smart fellow when he comes back – bursting to try out all he's learnt. You look out, Frederick!'

'It does sound funny when you call Fatty by his right name,' said Bets. 'Oooh, Fatty – let's hope we don't have a mystery after all, in case Mr Goon solves it instead of us.'

'Don't be silly,' said Pip. 'We can always get the better of Mr Goon. It's a pity something hasn't happened while he's been away – we could have solved it before he came back, without any interruptions from him.'

'Here's my small goddaughter,' said the Inspector, turning round to smile at a small girl in jodhpurs and riding jacket. 'Hello, Hilary. Won any prizes yet?'

Hilary sat on a fat little pony that didn't seem able to stand still. Buster kept well out of the way.

'Hello,' said Hilary. 'I'm going to ride now. I haven't won anything yet. Do you want to come and watch?'

'Of course,' said the Inspector. 'Let me introduce you to five friends of mine – who have helped me in many a difficult case. They want you and me to have a picnic tea with them. What about it?'

'Yes, I'd like to,' said Hilary, trying to stop her pony from backing on to an old gentleman nearby. 'Thank you.'

The pony narrowly missed walking on Buster. He yelped, and the restless little animal reared. Hilary controlled him and he tossed his head and knocked off the Inspector's trilby hat.

'Oh – sorry,' said Hilary, with a gasp. 'Bonny's a bit fresh, I'm afraid.'

'I quite agree,' said the Inspector, picking up

his hat before Bonny could tread on it. 'All right, Hilary – I'll come and watch you ride now – and we'll all have tea together when you've finished.'

Hilary cantered off, bumping up and down, her hair flying out under her jockey cap. Buster was most relieved to see her go. He ventured out from behind Fatty, saw a friend he knew and trotted over to pass the time of day; but what with horses of all sizes and colours rushing about he didn't feel at all safe.

It was a very pleasant afternoon. The policeman who had replaced Mr Goon while he was on holiday stood stolidly in a shady corner, and didn't even recognise the Inspector when he passed. It is true that Inspector Jenks was in plain clothes, but Bets felt that *she* would recognise him a mile off even if he was wearing a bathing costume.

'Afternoon, Tonks,' said the Inspector, as they passed the stolid policeman. He leapt to attention at once, and after that could be seen walking about very busily indeed. The Inspector there! Was there anything up? Were there pickpockets about – or some kind of hanky-panky anywhere? Tonks was on the lookout at once, and forgot all about standing comfortably in the shade.

Hilary didn't win a prize. Bonny really didn't behave at all well. He took fright at something and backed heavily into the judges, which made them look at him with much dislike and disfavour. Hilary was very disappointed.

She met them in a shady corner for tea, bringing Bonny with her. Buster growled. What? – that awful horse again! Bonny nosed towards him and Buster hastily got under a tent nearby, squeezing beneath the canvas.

Hilary was very shy. She would hardly say a word. She kept Bonny's reins hooked round one arm, which was just as well, as Bonny was really a very nosey kind of horse. Daisy kept a sharp eye on the baskets of food.

The Inspector talked away cheerfully. The children were disappointed that he had no cases to offer them, and no mystery to suggest.

'It's just one of those times when nothing whatsoever happens,' said Inspector Jenks, munching an egg-and-lettuce sandwich hungrily. 'No robberies, no swindlings, no crimes of any sort. Very peaceful.'

He waved his sandwich in the air as he spoke and it was neatly taken out of his hand by Bonny. Everyone roared at the Inspector's surprised face.

'Robbery going on nearby after all!' said Daisy. Hilary scolded Bonny, who backed away into the next picnic party. Buster put his nose out from under the tent canvas, but decided not to come out and join the party yet.

It was while all this was going on that the next mystery loomed up in the very middle of the picnic tea! Nobody expected it. Nobody realised it at first.

Pip happened to be looking down the field, where Mr Tonks, the policeman, was standing beside the Red Cross tent, having attended to somebody who had fainted in the heat. He stood there, mopping his forehead, probably feeling that he would be the next one to faint, when a man came quickly up to him. He looked like a gardener or handyman.

He spoke to Mr Tonks, who at once took out his black notebook, licked his thumb and flicked over the pages till he came to an empty one. Then he began to write very earnestly.

Pip saw this, but he didn't think anything of

17

it. But then Mr Tonks walked over to where Inspector Jenks was sitting with the Five Find-Outers and Hilary.

'Excuse me for interrupting, sir,' he said. 'But there's been a daylight robbery in Peterswood. I'll have to go and investigate, sir. Seems pretty serious.'

'I'll come with you,' said the Inspector, much to the disappointment of the children. He glanced round. 'Sorry,' he said. 'Duty calls, and all that! I may not see you again if I have to go straight back to my office. Thanks for a very fine tea. Good-bye, Hilary. You rode very well.'

He stepped straight back on to Bonny, who also backed up and pulled Hilary right over with the reins. In the general muddle, Fatty spoke to Mr Tonks, the policeman.

'Where was the robbery?' he asked.

'At Norton House,' said Mr Tonks. 'Up on the hill.'

'Don't know it,' said Fatty, disappointed. He stood up and spoke persuasively to the Inspector. 'I'll come along with you, sir, shall I? I – er – might be of a little help.'

'Sorry, Frederick – can't have you along just

now,' said the Inspector. 'It'll be a plain enough job, I expect – rather beneath your powers! If it's not – well, you'll get going on it, no doubt!'

He went off with Tonks. Fatty stared after them gloomily. Now they would be first on the job – they would see everything, notice everything. And when Mr Goon came back and took over from Mr Tonks, he would settle it all up and put a feather in his cap!

He sat down again. If only he could have gone to Norton House and had a snoop round himself! Now he really couldn't – the Inspector would be annoyed to see him there after he had said he didn't want him – and certainly the householders wouldn't allow him to look round all by himself, if he went after the Inspector had left.

'Never mind, Fatty,' said Bets, seeing how disappointed he was. 'It's only a silly little robbery, I expect. Nothing to bother about – no real mystery!'

Then something surprising happened. Hilary burst into tears! She wailed aloud and tears ran down her podgy cheeks.

'What's the matter? Do you feel sick?' asked Daisy, alarmed.

'No. Oh dear – it's *my* home that's been burgled!' wept Hilary. '*I* live at Norton House. Uncle Jenks must have forgotten it's where I live. Oh, what shall I do?'

Fatty rose to the occasion at once. He put his arm round the weeping Hilary. 'Now, now,' he said, producing an extremely clean white handkerchief, and wiping Hilary's face with it. 'Don't you worry. I'll take you home myself. I'll look after you. I'll even look all round your house to make sure there isn't a single robber left!'

'Oh, thank you,' said Hilary, still sniffing. 'I should hate to go home by myself.'

'We'd better wait a bit till your godfather has had time to look round himself,' said Fatty, who wasn't going to bump into the Inspector if he could help it.

'Then we'll go – and I'll soon see that everything is quite safe for you, Hilary!'

3. FATTY TAKES HIS CHANCE

The others looked at Fatty in admiration. *Some*how he always got what he wanted. Things always went right for him. He badly wanted to examine that burgled house, and he had been left behind by the Inspector – and, lo and behold, he could now go there, taking charge of Hilary, and nobody could say a thing against it!

'I can't go just yet,' sniffed Hilary. 'I've got to ride once more. You won't leave, will you? You *will* take me right home? You see, my parents are away, and there's only Jinny there – she's our housekeeper.'

Better and better! With no parents even to deal with, Fatty felt sure he could snoop as much as he wanted to. Larry and Pip looked at him rather jealously.

'We'll take Hilary home too,' said Larry.

'Better not,' said Fatty. 'Too many cooks

etcetera, etcetera.'

Hilary looked at him, wondering what he meant. The others knew all right. Hilary's tears began to fall again. 'It's my riding prizes I'm thinking of,' she explained, between sobs. 'My cups, you know. I've won so many. The burglar might have taken them.'

This talk about prizes seemed rather surprising to the others, who had no opinion at all of either Hilary or Bonny as regards horsemanship. Fatty patted her on the shoulder and gave her his enormous handkerchief again.

'I'll come up to your room with you and see if your things are safe,' said Fatty, feeling very pleased to think of the first-hand examination he could make. 'Now don't cry any more, Hilary.'

Bets looked on a little jealously. That silly little Hilary! Why did Fatty make such a fuss of her? Surely he would be ashamed of her, Bets, if *she* fussed like that?

'I'll come too, Fatty,' she said. Fatty was about to say no, when he thought that probably it would be a good idea to let Bets come – Hilary could show her this, that, and the other – and he could slip away unseen and snoop round by himself.

'Right, Bets,' he said. 'You can come – you'll be company for Hilary.' Bets was pleased. Now that silly little Hilary wouldn't have Fatty all to herself – she would see to that!

An enormously loud voice began calling over the field. 'Class Twenty-Two, please take your places, Class Twenty-Two.'

'That's my class,' said Hilary, scrambling to her feet. She pulled her cap straight and rubbed her eyes again. She brushed the crumbs off her jacket. Bonny neighed. He wanted to be off, now that he could see various horses moving about again. He had eaten as much tea as the others! He seemed to be an expert at nosing into baskets.

Hilary went off with Bonny, a podgy little figure with a tear-stained face. Fatty looked round triumphantly, winking at the others.

'I shall be in at the start, after all,' he said. 'Sorry you can't come, Pip, Larry and Daisy – but we can't all descend on the house. They'd smell a rat. Bets might be useful though – she can take up Hilary's attention while I'm looking round.'

Bets nodded. She felt proud to be in at the start

with Fatty. 'Shall we go after Hilary's ridden in this show?' she asked. Fatty considered. Yes – Mr Tonks and the Inspector should surely be gone by then.'

So, after Class Twenty-Two had competed in jumping, and Hilary had most surprisingly won the little silver cup offered, Fatty, Bets, and the rest moved off, accompanied by a suddenly-cheerful Hilary.

She rode Bonny, who, now that he had won something, seemed a little more sensible. The others walked beside her, till they came to the lane where Larry and Daisy had to leave them. Then a little later, Pip left them to go down the lane to his home. Fatty and Bets went on up the hill with Hilary. Buster kept sedately at Fatty's heels. He kept an eye on Bonny's legs and thought privately to himself that horses had been supplied with far too many hooves.

They came to Norton House. The Inspector's car was still outside. Blow! Fortunately, Hilary didn't want to go in the front way. She wanted to take Bonny to the stables, which were round at the back.

Bonny was led into his stable. 'Don't you rub him down or anything before you leave him?' asked Fatty. 'I'd be pleased to do it for you, Hilary.

You've had a tiring afternoon.'

Hilary thought that Fatty was the nicest boy she had ever met in her life. Fancy thinking of things like that! She wouldn't have been so much impressed if she had known how desperately Fatty was trying to stay down in the stables till the Inspector had gone!

Fatty groomed the pony so thoroughly that even Hilary was amazed. Bets watched with Buster, rather bored. 'See if they've gone,' whispered Fatty to her, jerking his head towards the front garden. Bets disappeared. She soon came back. She nodded. Fatty straightened up, relieved. Now he could stop working on that restless pony!

'Now we'll go to the house and find out exactly what happened,' said Fatty to Hilary. 'I expect your housekeeper is there. She'll tell us everything. Then you must show Bets all the prizes you have won. She'd love to see them. Wouldn't you, Bets?'

'Yes,' said Bets, doubtfully.

'You must see them too, Fatty,' said Hilary. He nodded – also doubtfully.

'Come along,' said Hilary and they walked up a long garden path to the house. It was a nice house, square-built, with plenty of windows. Trees surrounded it, and it could not be seen from the road.

They went in at the back door. A woman there gave a little scream of fright. 'Oh, lawks! Oh, it's you, Hilary. I'm in such a state of nerves, I declare I'd scream if I saw my own reflection in a mirror!'

Fatty looked at her. She was a little woman, with bright eyes and a good-tempered, sensible mouth. He liked her. She sank down into a chair and fanned herself.

'I've heard about the robbery,' said Hilary. 'Jinny, this is a boy who's brought me home and this is a girl called Bets. They are friends of my godfather, Inspector Jenks.'

'Oh, *are* they?' said Jinny, and Fatty saw that they had gone up in her estimation at once. 'Ah, he's a fine man, that Inspector Jenks. So patient and kind. Went over everything, he did, time and time again. And the questions he asked me! Well there now, you'd never think anyone could pour them out like that!'

'It must have been a great shock for you, Jinny,' said Fatty, in his most courteous and sympathetic

26

voice. He had a wonderful voice for that sort of thing. Bets looked at him in admiration. 'I was sorry for poor little Hilary too. I felt I really must see her home.'

'That was real gentlemanly of you,' said Jinny, thinking that Fatty was just about the nicest boy she had ever met. 'She's nervous, is Hilary. And I'll be nervous too, after this!'

'Oh, you don't need to be,' said Fatty. 'Burglars hardly ever come to the same place twice. Do tell us all about it – if it won't tire you too much.'

Jinny would not have been tired if she had told her story a hundred times. She began at once.

'Well, I was sitting here, half-asleep like, with my knitting on my knee – about four o'clock it must have been. And I was thinking to myself, "I must really get up and put the kettle on to boil," when I heard a noise.'

'Oooh,' said Hilary faintly.

'What sort of noise?' asked Fatty, wishing he could take out his notebook and put all this down. Still, if he forgot anything, Bets would remember it.

'A sort of thudding noise,' said Jinny. 'Out there

in the garden somewhere. Like as if somebody had thrown something out of the window and it had landed plonk in the garden.'

'Go on,' said Fatty, and Bets and Hilary listened, all eyes.

'Then I heard a cough upstairs somewhere,' said Jinny. 'A man's deep cough that was stifled quickly as if he didn't want to be heard. That made me sit up, I can tell you! "A man!" I ses to myself. "Upstairs and all! Can't be the master come back – anyway, that's not his cough." So up I gets, and I yells up the stairs, "If there's anybody up there that shouldn't be, I'm getting the police!" '

She paused and looked at the others, gratified to see their intense interest.

'Very very brave of you,' said Fatty. 'What happened next?'

'Well – I suddenly sees a ladder outside,' said Jinny, enjoying herself thoroughly. 'The gardener's ladder, it looked like – run up against the wall leading to the Mistress's bedroom. And I thinks to myself, "Aha! Mister Robber, whoever you are, I'll see you coming down that ladder! I'll take good notice of you too! If you've got a bunion on your toe, I'll notice it, and if you've got a squint in your eye, *I'll* know you again!" I know how important it is to notice what you can, you see.'

'Quite right,' said Fatty approvingly. 'And what *was* the robber like?'

'I don't know,' said Jinny, and she suddenly looked bewildered. 'He never came down that ladder after all!'

There was a pause. 'Well – how did he leave the house then?' asked Fatty. 'Did you hear him?'

'Never a sound,' said Jinny. 'I was standing in the hall, so I know he didn't come down the stairs – and there's only one set of stairs in this house. And there I stood, shivering and shaking I don't mind telling you – till I sees the telephone staring me in the face. And I grabs it and phones the police!'

'Go on,' said Fatty. 'What happened to the burglar? Was he still upstairs?'

'Well, just as I finished telephoning, who should come along but the baker and I yells to him, "Here you, come here and go upstairs with me. There's a burglar in the house." And the baker – he's a very very brave man for all he's so small – he came in and we went into every single room, and not a person was there. Not one!'

'He must have got out of another window,' said Fatty at last.

'He couldn't!' said Jinny triumphantly. 'They were all either shut and fastened, or there's a steep drop to the ground, enough to kill anyone taking a jump. I tell you, he had to come down the stairs or get down the ladder – and he didn't do either! There's a puzzle for you!'

'Well, he must still be there then,' said Fatty and Hilary gave a scream.

'He's not,' said Jinny. 'The Inspector, he looked into every hole and corner, even in the chest in your Ma's room, Hilary. I tell you what *I* think – he made himself invisible! Oh, laugh if you like – but how else could he have got away without me seeing him?'

4. PLENTY OF CLUES

Fatty asked Jinny a great many questions, and she seemed very pleased to answer them. Hilary got bored. 'Come on upstairs and see my riding prizes,' she said. 'Jinny, *those* didn't get stolen, did they?'

'No, Hilary dear – not one of them!' said Jinny comfortingly. 'I went to look, knowing as how you set such store on them. It's things like your Ma's little silver clock and some of the jewellery she left behind, and your father's cigarette box that have gone. All things from the bedrooms – nothing from downstairs that I can see.'

'Come on, Bets,' said Hilary, pulling Bets out of the room. 'Let's go upstairs. You come too, Fatty.'

Fatty was only too pleased. Hilary ran on ahead up the stairs. Fatty had a chance to whisper to Bets.

'You must pretend to be awfully interested, Bets, OK? That will give me a chance to slip away and have a snoop around.'

Bets nodded. She was bored with the horsey little Hilary, but she would do anything for Fatty. They all went upstairs. Hilary took them into her little room. Bets was quite astonished to see the array of cups and other prizes she had won. She began to ask all kinds of questions at once, so that Fatty might slip away.

'What did you win this cup for? What's this? Why are there two cups exactly the same? What's this printed on this cup?'

Hilary was only too anxious to tell her. Fatty grinned. He was soon able to slip away, with Buster trotting at his heels. He went into all the bedrooms. He noticed that in most of the rooms the windows were shut and fastened as Jinny had said. In Hilary's parents' room the window was open. Fatty went to it and looked out. A ladder led down from it to the ground.

That must be the ladder Jinny saw through the hall window, thought Fatty. I saw it myself as we went to the stairs. How did that thief get down from upstairs without being seen, if Jinny didn't see him come down the stairs or the ladder? He can't be here still, because the stolen goods are gone — and anyway, the place must have been thoroughly searched by the Inspector and Mr Tonks.

He went to see if there was any other window or balcony the thief could have dropped from unseen. But there wasn't.

Fatty concentrated his attention on the room from which the goods had been stolen. There were large dirty fingermarks on the wall by the window. Fatty studied them with interest.

The thief wore gloves — dirty gloves too, he thought. Well, he couldn't have been a very expert thief, to leave his prints like that! I'd better measure them.

He measured them. 'Big-handed fellow,' he said. 'Takes at least size eight-and-a-half in gloves, probably nines. Yes, must be nines, I should think. Hello, he's left his gloveprints here too — on the polished dressing-table.'

There were the same big prints again showing clearly. Fatty looked at them thoughtfully. It should be easy to pick out this thief — he really had very large hands.

He went to the window again. He leaned out

over the top of the ladder. 'He came up here by the ladder – didn't bother about the lower part of the house – he chucked the stuff out of the window – where did it land? Over there on that bed, I suppose. I'll go down and look. But yet, he didn't get *down* by the ladder? Why? Was he afraid of Jinny spotting him as he went down? He knew she was in the hall because he heard her shouting.'

Fatty pondered deeply. How in the world had the thief got away without being seen? It was true he could have slipped out of any of the other windows, but only by risking a broken leg, because there was such a steep drop to the ground – no ivy to cling to, no balcony to drop down to. Fatty went round the top part of the house again, feeling puzzled.

He came to a boxroom. It was very small and had a tiny window, which was fast-shut. Fatty opened it and looked down. There was a thick pipe outside, running right down to the ground.

Now – *if* the window had been open instead of shut – and *if* the thief had been even smaller than I am – so that he could have squeezed painfully out of this tiny window – he might have got down to the ground from here, thought Fatty. But the window's shut – and Jinny says all of them were, except the one with the ladder, and a few that nobody could leap from.

He went downstairs, hearing Hilary still talking soulfully about her cups. He couldn't hear a word from Bets. Poor Bets! She really was a great help.

'Who's that?' called Jinny sharply, as she heard Fatty come down the stairs.

'Only me,' said Fatty. 'Jinny, it's a puzzle how that thief got away without being seen, isn't it? Especially as he must have been rather a big fellow, judging from the size of his hands. I've been looking at all the windows. There's only one that has a pipe running by it down to the ground – the one in the boxroom – a tiny window. Was that shut?'

'Oh yes,' said Jinny. 'The Inspector asked me that same question. He said he found it shut too. And you're right – the thief couldn't possibly have squeezed out of that small window, he's too big. You should see his footprints out there on the bed – giant-size, I reckon!'

'I'll go and see, if you don't mind,' said Fatty.

Jinny didn't mind at all – she was only too pleased to let Fatty do anything – a nice, polite boy like that! You didn't come across them every day, more's the pity!

Fatty went out into the garden. He went to where the ladder was raised up against the house. He looked at the bed below. There were quite a lot of footprints there – certainly the thief had a large foot as well as large hands! Wears a shoe about size eleven or twelve, thought Fatty. Hm! Where's my measure?

Fatty measured a print and recorded it in his notebook. He also made a note of the pattern of the rubber heel that the thief wore on his boots – it showed clearly in the prints.

Then he went to where the thief had thrown the stolen goods. They had been thrown well away from the ladder, and had fallen in a bush, and on the ground around. Fatty poked about to see if he could find anything. He felt sure he wouldn't, because the Inspector had already been over the ground – and Fatty had a great respect for Inspector Jenks' ability to discover any clue left lying about!

He came across a curious print – large, roundish,

with criss-cross lines showing here and there. What could the thief have thrown out that made that mark? He went to ask Jinny.

'Ah, the Inspector, he asked me that too,' she said. 'And I couldn't tell him. There was nothing big taken as far as I know. I've seen the mark too – can't think what made it! It's a strange mark – roundish like that, and so big – big as my largest washing-up bowl!'

Fatty had measured the print and drawn it in his book, with the little criss-cross marks on it here and there. Funny. What could it be? It must have something to do with the robbery.

He shut his book. There was nothing more he could examine or find, he was sure of that. He was also sure that he hadn't discovered anything that the Inspector hadn't – probably he hadn't discovered so much! If the Inspector had found anything interesting, he would have taken it away. What a pity Fatty hadn't been on the spot with him when he came with Mr Tonks!

It won't be much of a mystery, I suppose, thought Fatty, going upstairs with Buster to fetch Bets. Surely a thief as large as this one will be easily found and caught. I shouldn't be surprised if the Inspector hasn't got him already!

This was rather a disappointing thought. Fatty went into Hilary's room and smiled when he saw poor Bets' bored face. She smiled back delightedly at him.

'Oh, Fatty – is it time to go? Hilary has been telling me all about her prizes.'

'Yes,' said Hilary, looking pleased with herself. 'Shall I tell *you* now, Fatty? See, this one was . . .'

'Oh, I've heard quite a lot, off and on,' said Fatty. 'You're wonderful, Hilary! To think you've won all those! You really must be proud.'

'Oh well . . .' said Hilary, trying to look modest. 'See, this one I . . .'

Fatty looked at his watch and gave such a loud exclamation that Bets jumped and Hilary stopped, startled.

'Good gracious! *Look* at the time! I shall have to see your prizes another time, Hilary. Bets, I must take you home – you'll get in an awful row if you're any later.'

Hilary looked disappointed. She had been quite prepared to go over the whole history of her riding prizes once again. Bets was overjoyed to think Fatty was at last going to leave.

'Thanks awfully, Hilary, for giving me such a lovely time,' said Bets politely but not very truthfully. Fatty patted Hilary on the shoulder and said it had been a real pleasure to meet her. Hilary beamed.

She went down to the front gate with them, and waved till they were out of sight. Bets heaved a sigh of relief when they at last turned a corner and the waving could no longer be seen.

'Oh, Fatty – did you find out anything? Is it a mystery?' she asked eagerly. 'Tell me!'

'I don't somehow think it is,' said Fatty. 'Just an ordinary little burglary, with one or two odd little touches – but I expect the Inspector and Mr Tonks have got more information than I have, actually, as they were there first. I'll go and see Mr Tonks, I think. He might let out something.'

'Why not ask the Inspector?' said Bets, as they turned down the lane to her home.

'Er – no – I think not,' said Fatty. 'I don't particularly want him to know I snooped round after all. Mr Tonks is the one to question. I'll see him tomorrow. Tell Pip I'll be round at eleven o'clock.'

He took Bets right up to the door of her house and said goodnight. 'And thanks for doing your bit for me,' he said. 'I know you were bored – but I couldn't have gone without you and snooped round – you were a real help.'

'Then I don't mind being bored,' said Bets. 'Oh dear – I never want to hear about riding prizes again!'

5. SOME INFORMATION FROM TONKS

Fatty went home and walked down to the shed at the bottom of the garden where he kept his most valuable possessions.

He cast an eye over the various chests and boxes in his closely guarded shed. Here he kept his disguises – old clothes of various kinds; hats, boots, and ragged scarves. Here was a box containing many curious things that he didn't want his mother either to find or to throw away! False teeth to put over his own – false cheek pads to swell out his face – eyebrows of all colours – wigs that fitted him and wigs that didn't – big and little moustaches. Oh, Fatty had a most interesting collection in this shed of his at the bottom of the garden!

He gazed at the array of belongings. I'd like to do a spot of disguising, he thought. I will when Mr Goon comes back. It's not much fun doing it now unless there's a mystery on, or Mr Goon to deceive. Wonder when he's coming back. I'll ask Mr Tonks tomorrow.

He went to see Tonks the very next morning at about ten o'clock. Buster ran beside his bicycle. Fatty had decided he really was too fat for words – exercise would be good for him. So poor Buster panted beside the bicycle, his tongue lolling out first on one side of his mouth and then on the other.

Fatty knocked at the door. 'Come in!' cried a voice and in went Fatty. He found Mr Tonks poring over a sheaf of papers. The stolid policeman looked up and nodded.

'Ah – Frederick Trotteville, isn't it? Great friend of the Inspector's, aren't you? He was telling me yesterday some of the things you'd done.'

This seemed a very good beginning. Fatty sat down. 'I don't know if you're too busy to spare me a minute,' he said. 'I took Hilary home last night, she was so scared, poor little thing – you know, the Inspector's goddaughter.'

'Oh – so that's what he meant when he suddenly said, "My word – Norton House – that's Hilary's home,"' said the policeman. 'I didn't like to ask him.'

'I expect he didn't realise it was his goddaughter's house that had been burgled when he went off with you,' said Fatty. 'Anyway, she was frightened and I took her home. I had a look round, of course – and I wondered if I'd found anything of use to you.'

'Shouldn't think so,' said Tonks. 'Not that I'm much of a one for solving cases – never have been – but the Inspector was there, you see, and there's nothing much *he* misses. Still, it's very nice of you to come along and offer to help.'

'Not at all,' said Fatty, in his most courteous voice. 'Er – did *you* find anything interesting?'

'Oh – just fingerprints – or, rather, gloveprints – and footprints,' said Tonks. 'Same as you did, I expect. Pretty big fellow, the thief seems to have been. Made a good getaway too – nobody saw him go, nobody met him down the hill – might have been invisible!'

Fatty laughed. 'That's what Jinny said. You'd have thought a big fellow like that, carrying a sack or parcel of some kind, would have been noticed, wouldn't you? Pity the baker didn't spot him when he arrived with the bread.'

'Yes. He never saw a thing,' said Tonks. 'I must say, it was pretty brave of him to go upstairs with Jinny and look around – he's a tiny little fellow, and wouldn't be any match for a big man. I went along to see him last night. He reckons his coming disturbed the thief. He hadn't really stolen very much, as far as I can make out.'

'Did anyone else come that afternoon – to Norton House, I mean?' asked Fatty.

'The postman, a woman delivering election leaflets, and a man selling logs, according to Jinny,' said Tonks. 'We've seen them all – they didn't notice anything out of the ordinary, not even the ladder. Anyway, they came a good time before the thief.'

'Where was the gardener?' asked Fatty.

'He'd gone off to take some tackle down to the gymkhana for Hilary,' said Tonks. 'He came back just as all the excitement was over. The baker sent him off to tell me about the robbery, so down he went to Petter's Field again.'

Fatty fell silent. This was a strange kind of thief – big, clumsy, easy to see – and yet apparently invisible! Not a soul had noticed him.

'Did you find any other clues?' asked Fatty. Tonks looked at him doubtfully. He had already said rather a lot to this polite and quite helpful boy. But ought he to tell him everything?

'You needn't worry about what you tell me,' said Fatty, seeing at once that Tonks had something else to say and wasn't sure about it. 'I'm a friend of the Inspector's – you know that. All I do is help if I can.'

'Yes. I know that,' said Tonks. 'The Inspector said, "Well, well – if *we* can't find the thief, Tonks, Frederick certainly will!" '

'Well, there you are,' said Fatty, grinning. '*You* haven't found him yet – so give me a chance, Mr Tonks.'

The policeman produced two dirty bits of paper. He handed them to Fatty, who looked at them with much interest. One had scribbled on it,

2 Frinton

The other was even shorter. It simply said,

1 Rods

'What do they mean?' asked Fatty, studying the dirty little scraps of paper.

'Don't know any more than you do,' said Tonks, taking them back. 'Number two, Frinton. Number one, Rods. Looks like addresses of some sort. But I'm not going off to Frinton or Rods, wherever they are, to hunt for the thief! We found these bits of paper near the bush where the stolen goods had been thrown.'

'Funny,' said Fatty. 'Do you think they've really anything to do with this case? They look like scraps of paper torn up by someone and thrown away.'

'That's what I said,' agreed Tonks. 'Anyway, I'll have to keep them, in case they're important.'

Fatty could see there was nothing else to find out from Tonks. He got up. 'Well – I wish you luck in finding the thief,' he said. 'It seems to me the only way to spot him will be to snoop round everywhere till we see a man wearing size twelve shoes and size nine gloves!'

Tonks gave a sudden grin. 'Well – if Mr Goon likes to do that, he's welcome. He's taking over the case when he comes back. Nice for him to have something to do in this dead-and-alive hole. I'm used to a big town – I don't like these quiet country places where the only thing that happens is a dog that chases sheep, or a man that doesn't buy his TV licence.'

Fatty could have told Tonks how wrong he was. He could have told him of all the extraordinary and exciting mysteries that had happened in Peterswood – but he didn't because of Mr Tonks' unexpected piece of news about Mr Goon.

'Did you say Mr Goon was coming back?' he asked. 'When?'

'You sound pleased,' said Tonks. 'I did hear you didn't like one another! He's coming back this afternoon. I hand over then. I won't be having any more to do with this case. Anyway, Mr Goon ought to put his hands on the thief soon enough – he can't be far away.'

Fatty glanced at the clock on the mantelpiece. He must go, or he would keep the others waiting. He had found out all he wanted to know – though it wasn't much help really. And Mr Goon was coming back! Old Mr Goon. Clear-Orf, with his bombastic ways and his immense dislike of all the Five Find-Outers and their doings – to say nothing of Buster!

Fatty shook hands solemnly with Tonks, assured him that it had been a great pleasure to meet him, and went off on his bicycle, with Buster panting once again near the pedals.

The others were waiting for him in Pip's garden. It was very hot again, and they lay on their backs with iced lemonade in a patch of shade.

'Here's old Fatty,' said Pip, hearing his bicycle bell ringing as Fatty came at sixty miles an hour up the drive. 'How in the world can he ride at that pace when it's so hot?'

But Fatty was the bringer of news, and he didn't think once about the heat as he came riding up the garden path to the others. He flung his bicycle down and beamed round at them all.

'Mr Goon's coming back,' he said. 'This afternoon! *And* he'll take over the case of the invisible thief – so we shall have some fun.'

Everyone sat up at once. 'That's good news,' said Larry, who always enjoyed their tussle of wits with Mr Goon. 'Did you see Mr Tonks then? Had he anything to say?'

Fatty sat down. 'Not much,' he said. 'He and the Inspector didn't really find out any more than I did.

I'll tell you what I found out yesterday in a minute – unless Bets has already told you?'

No, Bets hadn't. She had thought that Fatty ought to tell everything – so he got out his notebook and went into all the details of the new case.

He told them of the setting-up of the ladder – the large footprints in the bed below – the equally large gloveprints in the bedroom above – the throwing out of the stolen goods – the apparently completely invisible getaway.

'Only two ways of escape – down the ladder or down the stairs,' said Fatty. 'And Jinny, the housekeeper, was standing in the hall, where she could see both – and she swears nobody came down either stairs or ladder.'

'Must have got out of another upstairs window then,' said Pip.

'All either fastened and shut, or too far from the ground,' said Fatty. 'There's only one that might have been used – and that is a tiny window in a boxroom – there was a fat pipe running by it to the ground. Anyone could have slithered down that – if he was tiny enough to get out of the window! But – the window was shut and fastened when

Jinny went round the upstairs part of the house.'

'Hmm – well, no thief could squeeze out of a window, hold on to a pipe, and then shut and fasten the window after him – from the inside!' said Pip. 'It's a bit of a puzzle, isn't it? Jinny's right – the man's invisible!'

'Well, if he is, he'll certainly perform again,' said Larry. 'I mean – an invisible thief has a great advantage, hasn't he!'

Fatty laughed. He showed them his notebook with the drawings of the footprints, the gloveprints – and the curious round-shaped print with the faint criss-cross marks.

'Can't imagine what made *that* mark,' he said. 'It was near the bush where the stolen goods were thrown. And look – can anyone make anything of this?'

He showed them the curious addresses – if they were addresses – that he had copied into his notebook too.

'"2 Frinton". "1 Rods",' he said. 'Those words and numbers were found on two separate dirty scraps of paper near the bush. What on earth do they mean?'

'Frinton,' said Bets, wrinkling her forehead in a frown. 'Wait a minute. That rings a bell, somehow. Frinton, Frinton. *Frinton!* Where have I heard that lately?'

'Oh – one of your friends sent you a postcard from Frinton-on-Sea, I expect, silly,' said Pip.

'No. Wait a minute – I'm remembering!' said Bets. 'It's that place down by the river – not very far from here, actually – the place where they take visitors – Frinton Lea!'

'Clever old Bets,' said Fatty, admiringly. 'There may be something in that. If we find a large-sized fellow slouching about there, we'll keep a watch on him.'

'What about "1 Rods",' said Larry.

Nobody could think up anything for that.

'We'll go round looking at the names of houses and find out if anyone has that name,' said Fatty. 'Rods. It's a peculiar name, anyhow. Well, Find-Outers – the mystery has begun!'

6. THE SECOND ROBBERY

Mr Goon arrived back that afternoon, bursting with importance. His refresher course and the things he had learnt at it had given him completely new ideas about his job. Ah, he knew a lot more about the ways of wrongdoers now! He knew a good deal more about how to catch them. And he also knew an enormous amount about the art of disguising himself.

It was entirely because of Fatty that Mr Goon had applied himself to the course given in the arts of disguise. Fatty had bewildered, puzzled, angered and humiliated poor Mr Goon so many times because of his artful disguises. The times that boy had turned up as a red-headed cheeky telegraph boy – or an old man – or even a voluble and rude old woman!

Mr Goon gritted his teeth whenever he thought

of them. Now – NOW – Mr Goon himself knew a bit about disguises, and he had brought back with him quite a remarkable collection of clothes and other gadgets.

He'd show that fat fellow he wasn't the only one to use disguises. Mr Goon patted his pocket as he travelled home by coach. Greasepaint – eyebrows – a beard – a wig – he was bringing them all back. He'd trick that toad properly. A real toad, that was what that boy was.

Mr Goon was most delighted to hear about the new robbery from Mr Tonks. Ah – here was something he could get his teeth into at once. With all the new things he had learnt, he could tackle this fresh case easily – finish with it long before Fatty had even begun it.

He was a little upset to find that Fatty had apparently already heard about it and was interested in it. 'That boy!' he growled to Tonks. 'Can't keep his nose out of anything!'

'Well, he couldn't very well help it this time,' said Tonks stolidly. 'He was there when I went and reported the robbery to the Inspector.'

'He would be,' said Goon, scowling. 'Look

here, Mr Tonks – I tell you this – if the Crown Jewels were stolen one dark night, that boy would somehow know all about it – he'd be there!'

'Rather far-fetched, that,' said Tonks, who thought Mr Goon was a bit of a turnip-head. 'Well, I'll be going. I've given you all the details – you've got those scraps of paper, haven't you? With those addresses on?'

'Yes. I'm going to do something about those at once,' said Goon pompously. 'I reckon if those places are watched, something'll come out – and watched they will be.'

'Right,' said Tonks. 'Well, good-bye Mr Goon. Good luck.'

He went off and Goon heaved a sigh of relief. He sat down to look through the papers that Tonks had left.

But he hadn't been studying them long before the telephone rang. Goon picked up the receiver and put it to his ear. 'Police here,' he said gruffly.

Someone spoke volubly and excitedly at the other end. Goon stiffened as he listened – ah – another robbery – things were getting interesting!

'I'll be along, madam. Leave everything as it

is. Don't touch a thing,' commanded Goon in his most official voice. He put on his helmet and went out to get his bicycle.

And this time those interfering children won't be there to pester me, he thought, as he cycled quickly along in the heat. I'll be in first on this.

He cycled through the village, turned up a side road, and came to a house. He got off his bicycle, wheeled it in at the gate, and went up to the front door.

It was opened by Fatty!

Mr Goon gaped. He scowled. He couldn't think of a word to say. Fatty grinned.

'Good afternoon, Mr Goon,' he said, in his politest voice, a voice that always infuriated Mr Goon. 'Come in. We've been expecting you.'

'What are *you* doing here?' said Mr Goon, finding his voice at last. 'Tricking me? Getting me here for nothing? I thought it all sounded a bit funny on the phone – silly sort of voice, and silly sort of tale. I might have guessed it was one of your tricks – just to welcome me home, I suppose! Well – you'll be sorry for this. I'll report you! You think because the Inspector is friendly to you, you can get away with anything! You think . . .'

'Woof!' said somebody – and Buster darted out in ecstasy, so pleased to hear the voice of his old enemy that he wagged his tail for joy! That was enough for Goon. He departed hurriedly, muttering as he went, his bicycle wobbling down the path.

'Well!' said Fatty, in surprise. 'What's up with him? He can't *really* think I'm hoaxing him! Larry, come here. Mr Goon's gone off his head!'

Larry and Daisy appeared. They looked after the departing Mr Goon, who was now sailing out of the gate.

'He's gone,' said Fatty. 'He came – he saw – and he didn't stay to conquer. What's up with him?'

'You'd have thought that with another robbery, he'd have stayed like a shot,' said Daisy.

'Well, Lucy reported it fully,' said Fatty. 'I heard her on the telephone.'

Somebody called out to them. 'Was that the police? Tell them to come in here.'

'It was Mr Goon,' said Fatty. 'He came – but he went at once. Funny.'

'Well, thank goodness you and Larry and Daisy are here,' said Mrs Williams. 'I don't know what I should have done without you.'

It had all happened very suddenly indeed. Fatty had gone to tea with Larry and Daisy that afternoon, as Pip and Bets had gone out with their mother. They had been having tea in the garden, when someone from the house next door began to call for help.

'Help! Robbers! Help! Help, I say!'

'Gosh – that's Mrs Williams yelling,' said Larry, getting up quickly. 'Our next door neighbour.'

'What's happened?' asked Daisy, half-frightened at the continual shouts.

'She's been robbed,' said Fatty. 'Come on – quick!'

All three climbed over the fence and appeared in the next door garden. Mrs Williams saw them from a window and beckoned. 'Come in, quickly! I'm scared!'

They rushed in at the back door. There was no one in the kitchen. A heap of groceries lay on the table, and four loaves sat neatly side by side. A parcel stood by the door.

Fatty's quick eyes noted everything as he ran through the kitchen into the hall. 'Kitchen door open – the thief went in there, probably. Wonder if it's the same one as yesterday.'

Mrs Williams was sitting on her sofa, looking rather white. She was a gentle, grey-haired old lady, and she was very frightened. 'Get me my smelling-salts out of my bag,' she said faintly to Daisy. Daisy got them and she held them to her nose.

'What happened, Mrs Williams?' said Fatty.

'Well, I was having my afternoon rest in here,' said Mrs Williams. 'And I suddenly heard the sound of heavy footsteps upstairs. Then I heard the sound of a deep, hollow sort of cough – rather like a sheep makes, really.'

'A hollow cough?' said Fatty at once, remembering that Jinny had also heard the same noise.

'Yes. I sat up, scared,' said Mrs Williams. 'I crept out of this room and went into the hall. And suddenly someone gave me a push into the cupboard there, and in I went. The door was locked on me, and I couldn't get out.'

Just as she was speaking, there came the sound of a key in the front door, and then the door was opened and shut. 'Who's that?' asked Fatty.

'Oh, that's Lucy, my companion – Miss Lucy,'

said Mrs Williams. 'Oh, I'm glad she's back. Lucy, Lucy, come here. A dreadful thing has happened!'

Miss Lucy came in. She was a little bird-like woman with very sharp eyes, and a funny bouncy way of walking. She went to Mrs Williams at once.

'What is it? You look pale!'

Mrs Williams repeated what she had told the children. They waited patiently till she came to where she had been locked in the cupboard.

'Well, there I was in the hall cupboard, and I could hear the thief walking about overhead again,' said Mrs Williams. 'Heavy-footed too, and clumsy by the way he knocked things over. Then he came downstairs – I heard him clearly because the stairs pass over the hall cupboard – and I heard that awful sheep-like cough again.'

She stopped and shuddered.

'Go on,' said Fatty gently. 'How did you get out of the cupboard? Did the thief unlock it?'

'He must have,' said Mrs Williams. 'I was so scared when I heard him coming downstairs that I must have fainted – and when I came round again, I found myself lying in a heap on all the boots and shoes and golf-clubs – and the door was unlocked!

I tried it – and it opened.'

'Hmmmm!' said Fatty. 'Miss Lucy, you'd better telephone the police, I think – and I'll take a little look round. This is very – very – interesting!'

7. MR GOON ON THE JOB

Miss Lucy ran to telephone the police at once and, as we know, got on to Mr Goon. Very excitedly and volubly she told him all that had happened, and then the household waited for Mr Goon to arrive.

Fatty took a hasty look round while they waited. He was sure the thief was the same as the one who had been to Norton House the day before. For one thing – that deep, hollow cough – and for another, the heavy-footed clumsiness sounded as if they belonged to the same burglar.

Fatty ran upstairs. The first thing he saw in one of the bedrooms was a print on the wall, just by the door – a large gloveprint! He flicked open his notebook and compared it with the measurements detailed there. Yes – pretty much exactly the same.

Now what about any footprints in the garden?

The ground was so dry now that, unless the thief obligingly walked on a flower-bed, he probably wouldn't leave any prints.

Fatty was just going out to see, when he caught sight of Mr Goon coming up the front drive, and went to the door. *What* a shock it would be for Mr Goon to see him! Fatty really enjoyed opening the door.

He was surprised when Mr Goon dashed off so soon. Surely he couldn't be idiotic enough to really think that Fatty had hoaxed him? Well, well – if so, then he, Fatty, might as well get on with his job of snooping round. Mr Goon wouldn't have let him do that if he had taken charge of the case, that was certain.

So Fatty made hay while the sun shone and slipped out into the garden, leaving Larry and Daisy to try and explain Mr Goon's sudden departure to Mrs Williams and Miss Lucy. They were most indignant.

Fatty went out through the kitchen door. He had decided that the thief had come in that way, as the front door had been shut. He went down the path that led from the kitchen. He saw a bed of flowers and walked over to it. The bed was underneath the sitting-room window, and it was in that room that Mrs Williams had been asleep.

Fatty gave an exclamation. On the bed were a couple of very large footprints. The same ones as yesterday – he was sure of it! He flicked open his notebook again.

The bed was drier than the one he had examined the day before for prints, and the rubber heel did not show this time – but the large prints were there, plain to see.

The thief came and looked in at the window, thought Fatty. And he saw Mrs Williams fast asleep. Hello – here are some more prints – on this bed. Why did he walk here?

There didn't seem any reason why the thief had walked on the second bed – but it was clear that the prints matched the others. In fact, everything matched – the gloveprints, the footprints, the hollow cough. Would there also be any mark like that big, roundish one that Fatty had seen at Norton House?

He hunted about for one; and he found it! It was very faint, certainly, and the criss-cross marks could hardly be seen. The roundish print was by the kitchen door, on the dusty path there. Something had been stood there – what was it?

Any scraps of paper this time? wondered Fatty, rather struck by the way that everything seemed to be repeated in this second case of robbery. He hunted everywhere – but there were no scraps of paper this time.

He went indoors, and met Miss Lucy coming out to find him. 'Mr Goon has just telephoned,' she said. 'I can't make him out. He wanted to know if there had been a *real* robbery here! Well, why didn't he stay and ask us about it when he came? He must be mad.'

Fatty grinned. Mr Goon had evidently thought the whole thing over and decided that he had better find out for certain what the truth was – and, to his disgust, he had found that the robbery was real – it wasn't a trick of Fatty's after all!

'He's a bit of a turnip-head,' said Fatty cheerfully. 'Never mind. You tell him I'm on the job when he comes – he needn't worry about it at all. I've got it well in hand.'

Miss Lucy looked doubtfully at Fatty. She was

getting a little bewildered, what with thieves, and policemen who arrived and departed all in the same minute, and boys who seemed to be acting like policemen ought to, but didn't.

Fatty pointed to the groceries on the table. 'Who took these in?' he asked. 'Have you a cook?'

'Yes. But she's off for the day,' said Miss Lucy. 'I left the back door open for the grocer's girl to leave the groceries in the kitchen – she often does that for us. The baker's been too, I see – and the postman, because there's a parcel by the door. Mrs Williams has been in all afternoon, but she likes a nap, so the tradesmen never ring when Cook is out. They just leave everything, as you see.'

'Yes, I see,' said Fatty thoughtfully. He gazed at the groceries, the bread, and the parcel. Three people had come to the house in a short time. Had one of them noticed the thief hanging about anywhere? He must find out.

Mr Goon arrived again, a little shamefaced. Miss Lucy let him in, looking rather severe. She thought a policeman who behaved like Mr Goon was ridiculous.

'Er – sorry I didn't come in before,' said Mr

Goon. 'Hope I've not kept you waiting too long, er – urgent business, you know. By the way – that boy – has he gone?'

'If you mean young Trotteville, he is still here, examining everything,' said Miss Lucy coldly. 'He told me to tell you not to bother about the job. He's got it well in hand. I am sure he will recover the jewellery Mrs Williams has had stolen.'

Goon turned a curious purple colour, and Miss Lucy felt rather alarmed. She felt that she didn't want this peculiar policeman in the house at all. She tried to shut the front door – but Goon put his enormous foot in the crack at once.

Miss Lucy gave a faint shriek, and Mr Goon took his foot out again, trying to think of something reassuring to say to this aggravating, bird-like creature.

Miss Lucy promptly shut the door and even put up the chain. Goon stared at the door, and went purple again. He walked ponderously round to the back door, where he found Fatty examining the path for footprints.

'Gah!' said Mr Goon, in a tone of deep disgust. 'Can't get rid of you! First you're at the front door, now you're at the back door. You be off. This here case has got nothing to do with you. Nothing.'

'That's where you're wrong, Mr Goon,' said Fatty in the mild, courteous voice that made Goon see red. 'I was called in to help. I've found out a lot already.'

Larry and Daisy heard Goon's infuriated voice and came out through the kitchen to listen. They stood at the back door, grinning.

'You here too?' said Goon, in even greater disgust. 'Can't you keep your noses out of anything? Now, you clear orf, all of you, and let me get on with my work here. And just you call off that dog!'

Buster had now joined the trio, and was capering delightedly round Mr Goon's feet.

'He's missed his ankle-hunting,' Fatty explained. 'Don't grudge him a little fun, Mr Goon. And don't you kick him. If you do, I won't call him off.'

Mr Goon gave it up. He pushed past Larry and Daisy, went into the kitchen, still pursued by a delighted Buster, and through the door into the hall. By a clever bit of work, he managed to shut the door of the kitchen on Buster, who scraped at it, barking wildly.

'Well, he's gone to do a spot of interviewing,' said Fatty, sitting down on the kitchen doorstep. 'He won't find the two ladies very pleased with him, I fear. He's rather started off on the wrong foot with them.'

'Fatty, have you found out anything interesting?' asked Larry eagerly. 'I saw you with your measuring tape, out of the window. What have you discovered?'

'I've discovered exactly the same as I discovered yesterday,' said Fatty. 'Except that I haven't found any bits of paper with names and numbers on. Look at those prints over there.'

Larry and Daisy examined them with interest. 'I know only one person in this village with feet big enough to fit those prints,' said Daisy. Fatty looked up at once.

'Who? Perhaps you've hit on the very person! There can't be many people with such enormous feet.'

'Well – it's Mr Goon – old Clear-Orf!' said Daisy with a giggle. The others roared.

'You're right. His feet would certainly fit those

prints!' said Fatty. 'Unfortunately, he's about the only large-footed person who's absolutely ruled out.'

'We'll certainly have to go about with our eyes on people's feet,' said Larry. 'It's the one thing the thief can't hide! He can stick his great hands in his pockets and stop his hollow cough – but he can't hide his great feet!'

'No – you're right,' said Fatty. 'Well, let's not stop any more. Mr Goon's had about enough of us for one afternoon, I should think.'

They climbed over the fence into Larry's garden. Buster squeezed through a hole.

'Gosh – I'd forgotten we were in the middle of tea,' said Fatty, pleased to see the remains of sandwiches and cakes on the grass. 'What's happened to some of these potted-meat sandwiches? Your cat's been at them, Larry.'

'Buster – on guard!' said Larry at once, and Buster growled and looked round for the cat.

They finished their tea, talking about the two robberies. After a time, Buster growled again and went to the fence. 'Must be Mr Goon over the other side, doing a spot of detecting,' said Fatty with a grin. 'Let's go and see his turnip-brains at work.'

Goon was busy looking for prints and clues. He was most irritated to see three heads looking over the wall at him. They watched him solemnly as he measured and marked.

'Look! He's found a footprint!' said Larry, in an admiring voice. The back of Mr Goon's neck went scarlet but he said nothing.

'Now he's measuring it,' said Daisy. 'Oooh, isn't he *care*ful?'

'Brains, Daisy, brains,' said Fatty. 'What can we do against brains like that?'

Mr Goon felt as if he was going to burst. Those children! Toads! Pests! Always in his way, buzzing round like a lot of mosquitoes. He made a very dignified retreat into the kitchen, rather hurried at the end when he discovered that Buster had squeezed through the hole in the fence and was after him.

'Clear orf!' he shouted, slamming the door in Buster's face. 'You clear orf!'

8. FATTY MAKES SOME PLANS

Fatty called a meeting down in his shed the very next day. Larry and Daisy arrived punctually, and Pip and Bets soon after. Buster greeted them all exuberantly, as if he hadn't seen them for years.

'This is a proper meeting,' announced Fatty. 'An official one, I mean. We've got our mystery all right – and we've got just under four weeks to solve it. That ought to be plenty of time!'

'Yes, it ought – for old hands like us!' said Larry, grinning. 'Did you tell Pip and Bets all about yesterday's robbery next door to us? Do they know everything?'

'Yes. I went to tell them last night,' said Fatty. 'We've got to make plans this morning.'

'What? Lists of suspects and so on?' asked Bets eagerly.

'We haven't got a single suspect,' said Fatty. 'Not

71

one! It's about the only mystery we've ever had with two crimes and no suspects at all. Most extraordinary. It's going to be difficult to get on with the case till we find a few suspects to enquire about.'

'We've got plenty of clues,' said Daisy. 'Footprints – gloveprints – coughs – bits of paper . . .'

'What's your plan, Fatty?' asked Pip. 'I bet you've got one.'

'Well, I have, as a matter-of-fact,' said Fatty modestly. 'It's like this – all we've got to go on at the moment is what we think the thief looks like – big-footed, heavy-handed, clumsy, with a deep, hollow cough – and we've got two bits of paper possibly dropped by him – and if they are addresses or names, which they probably are, we must watch those addresses or people.'

'Yes,' said Larry. 'And what about asking the grocer, the baker, and the postman if they saw any sign of a big-footed fellow yesterday afternoon, when they delivered their goods in our road?'

'I was coming to that,' said Fatty. 'It seems to me we must split up a bit and each do a job, as we usually do.'

'Oh dear,' said Bets. 'I'm really not much good by myself.'

'You're one of the best of us,' said Fatty warmly, and Bets blushed with pleasure. 'Who solved the mystery of the pantomime cat, I'd like to know? You did, Bets – oh yes you did – without your bright idea about it we'd never have solved it! So just you do your bit this time too.'

'Oh, I will, Fatty,' said Bets earnestly.

'Now you, Larry, go and interview the postman,' said Fatty. 'And you, Pip, go to the baker. If he's the same one that Jinny at Norton House called in to help her, the one who searched the upstairs rooms for her, all the better. He may have noticed something about the two cases that we haven't.'

'Right,' said Pip. 'I believe he is *our* baker too.'

'And you, Daisy and Bets, go and interview the grocer's girl,' said Fatty. 'Apparently it's a girl who delivers Harris's goods – that's the grocer. Go and get her to talk – listen to all she says – remember it, and we'll piece together everything when we meet again.'

There was a silence. Everyone wondered what little job Fatty had kept for himself.

'What are *you* going to do?' asked Bets.

'I'm going to disguise myself,' said Fatty, and Bets gave a squeal of joy. 'And I'm going to go and watch Frinton Lea, just to see if any big-footed fellow lives there! If I watch the house all day long, I may see something.'

'But, Fatty – you'll be noticed if you stand outside all day long,' said Daisy. 'Besides – what about meals?'

'I've thought of all that,' said Fatty. 'Leave it all to me! I won't tell you my disguise. When you've done your jobs, you can come along and see if you recognise me. I'll be within fifty yards of the house all day long – visible to everyone – but I bet you anything you like that nobody will pay a moment's attention to me!'

They all stared at him. He stared back, his eyes twinkling. 'We shall spot you at once,' said Daisy.

'All right. Spot me then,' said Fatty. 'Now, come on – let's get going. Clear orf, all of you – and let me disguise myself!'

They all went off, laughing, wondering what Fatty was going to do. They were absolutely certain that they would spot Fatty at once. So would everyone else notice him? How could anyone loiter outside a house all day long without being noticed? And what about meals? There was nowhere down by Frinton Lea where he could even have a snack. There were fields behind and the river ran just in front.

'I'm going back home to wait for the baker,' said Pip. 'He comes to us about twelve o'clock, I think.'

'Oh, that's an awfully good idea,' said Larry. 'I'll come with you, and wait for the parcel postman to come to your house too. Then we can keep each other company.'

'He may not come,' said Pip. 'We don't always have parcels.'

'I'll have to chance that,' said Larry. 'I don't feel like going to the post office and asking to interview the parcel postman there, in front of everyone! I half thought I'd have to do that at first!'

'What about the grocer's girl?' said Daisy. 'Do you have Harris for your grocer, Pip? If you do, Bets and I can be with you and Larry, and we can all be together.'

'No, we don't have Harris,' said Pip. 'Let me see

now – what roads does the girl deliver to in the mornings? I've seen her somewhere. I know she only goes to your part of the town in the afternoon.'

'I know! She delivers down the other end of the town,' said Bets suddenly. 'I was at Mrs Kendal's once, with a message for Mummy – and the grocer's girl came then. We could go and wait about for her there, Daisy.'

'Right. Come on,' said Daisy. 'Good-bye, boys – don't start playing a game and forget all about your job!'

'Don't be silly, Daisy,' said Larry, quite annoyed. The boys went off to Pip's and the girls went off to the other end of the town.

They were lucky because they didn't have to wait very long. They sat in the small dairy near Mrs Kendal's, eating ice creams, keeping a watch for the grocer's van.

'There it is!' said Bets suddenly, and Daisy looked up to see Harris's yellow van coming round the corner. It came to a stop nearby.

Daisy and Bets paid quickly for their ice creams and hurried out. They were just in time to see the grocer's girl jump from the van, hurry to the back, undo the door, and drag out a big box piled with groceries.

'Let her go in with it first, and then we'll speak to her when she comes out,' said Daisy. They walked slowly to the back of the van. Then Bets saw that a little packet of soap powder had fallen out and was lying in the road.

'It must have fallen out of the girl's box,' she said to Daisy, and bent to pick it up just as the grocer's girl came out again, this time with her box empty.

'You dropped this,' said Bets, holding it out.

'Oh, thanks very much,' said the girl gratefully. 'I missed it when I took the things in just now. I'm in an awful hurry this morning – had an interview with the police, you know. About the robbery at Mrs Williams'.'

This was just the opening the other two wanted. Daisy seized on it eagerly. 'Oh, did you really? Did you know that my brother and I live next door to Mrs Williams, and we rushed in to help her?'

'No! Well I never!' said the girl, astonished. 'Did you see anything of the thief? I hear he took quite a bit of Mrs Williams' jewellery.'

'Did he?' said Daisy, who hadn't heard yet what exactly had been taken. '*You* went to the house yesterday afternoon too, didn't you? Did *you* see anything of the thief?'

'No, not a thing,' said the girl. 'I didn't see anyone at all. I think I must have come before he was there. I never saw or heard anything.'

'Did you see any loaves or any parcel in the kitchen when you went in?' asked Bets, wondering if the grocer's girl had gone to the house before the others.

'There were no loaves there when I went, and I didn't see any parcel,' said the girl, getting into her van. 'Mr Goon asked me a lot of questions this morning – and I couldn't tell him a thing. To think I was there and might have brushed against the robber! Well, it just shows, doesn't it?'

Bets and Daisy didn't know exactly what it showed, but they nodded their heads.

'Sorry I can't stop,' said the girl. 'I'd love to hear what you did too – but I'm so very late. To think I didn't hear or see a *thing*. Bad luck, wasn't it?'

She drove off. Daisy and Bets looked at one

another. 'Well, that was unexpectedly easy,' said Bets. 'It took us hardly any time. We may as well go back and see how the boys are getting on.'

So they went off to the boys, who were patiently waiting for the postman and the baker. They were swinging on the gate so as not to miss them. They looked most surprised to see Daisy and Bets so soon.

'We had an easy job,' said Daisy. 'But nothing came of it. The grocer's girl delivered her goods before the others, and she didn't see or hear anything suspicious at all.'

'Nobody ever seems to see this thief,' said Larry. 'They hear him and see his footmarks and glovemarks, but they don't see him. I bet neither the postman nor the baker will have seen him either.'

'Here *is* the postman!' said Daisy. 'Look – coming up the road on his little cycle van. Let's hope he's got a parcel for your house, Pip.'

The postman delivered two parcels next door. He came out again, mounted his saddle, and pedalled slowly to Pip's house. He stopped. He rummaged in his little van and produced a parcel.

'Mrs Hilton,' he read out and looked at the children. 'Any of you a Hilton?'

'Yes, I am,' said Pip, going over to the van. 'I'll take it to my mother. It'll save you a long ride up the drive and back.'

'Thanks,' said the postman. 'Sign for it, will you?'

Pip signed. 'I hope you won't bump into a thief today,' he said, giving the postman back his stump of a pencil. 'I hear you almost ran into one yesterday!'

'Yes,' said the postman. 'Mr Goon the policeman has been trying to find out if I saw him. I didn't. I went to the back door, as the Cook had told me to, so as not to disturb Mrs Williams – and I saw all the groceries on the table, and I left my parcel by the door.'

'Were there any loaves on the table too?' asked Larry.

'Not as far as I remember,' said the postman. 'I just popped my hand in with the parcel and popped out again. I was in a hurry. I didn't see or hear anything at all. Off I went. I don't know whether the thief was there then or not – skulking round maybe – or hiding in a bush.'

He began to pedal slowly away. The children watched him go.

'Nobody's much help,' said Pip. 'I never knew such a thief for not being noticed by anyone. You'd think they'd see his big feet, anyhow, wouldn't you?'

'Now we'll wait for the baker,' said Larry. 'Then we'll scoot off down to Frinton Lea and spot Fatty. I *bet* we spot him. Even if he's disguised himself as a tree, we'll spot him.'

'Hurry up, baker!' said Bets, swinging on the gate. 'You're the last one left – and I guess you won't have noticed the thief either!'

9. THE PECULIAR FISHERMAN

The baker arrived at last. He was a cocky little bantam of a man, with a rather high voice, and a silly way of clearing his throat. He left his van at the bottom of the road and came along carrying his basket on his arm.

'Hello, kids,' he said, as he came up to the gate. 'Having a swing-swong, eh?'

'Shall we take the bread to our cook for you?' asked Pip.

'Well – there are thieves about, you know!' said the baker, pretending to look scared. 'My word – I nearly ran into one yesterday, up at Mrs Williams'. Did you hear about that?'

'What happened?' asked Larry, thinking it would be a good thing to let him talk.

'Well, nothing really as far as I'm concerned,' said the baker. 'I goes up there as usual, carrying my bread on my arm in my basket, like I always does. I knocks on the kitchen door before I remembers that Cookie is out. I sees the groceries on the table, and a parcel by the door, and I says, "Ah, the grocer girl's been and left her things, and so's the postman. Now it's your turn, baker!" '

He grinned at them as if he had said something rather clever.

'And so I looks at the note Cookie's left for me, and I sees as how she wants four loaves,' went on the cocky little baker. 'And I pops them down, and out I goes.'

'And you didn't see or hear anything of the thief at all then,' said Larry, disappointed.

'No. Nothing,' said the baker. 'All I see is some big footprints on a bed.'

'Ah – you saw those!' said Pip and Larry together. The baker looked surprised.

'What do *you* know about them?' he said. 'Yes, I see them – and I thinks – ah, somebody's been walking their big feet all over the beds. Maybe the window-cleaner or somebody. And off I goes.'

'That means that the thief must either have come and gone, or was still there, hiding somewhere while you were delivering your bread,' said Larry. 'Gosh – you might easily have seen him. What a pity you didn't.'

'I never seen him the other day either, at Norton House,' said the baker in his high, rather silly voice. 'I heard Jinny shouting and in I went – but we didn't see no thief at all.'

'Funny,' said Pip, puzzled. 'Well, baker – if you'd like to give me your basket, I'll take it up to our cook and let her see what bread she wants. It will save you a long walk up the drive.'

He held out his hand for the basket, but the baker backed away and shook his head.

'No thanks. I don't want boys messing about with my nice clean bread,' said the baker. 'I'm particular, I am. I'm the only baker in Peterswood that covers his bread up with a clean cloth.'

'Oh, all right,' said Pip. 'Take it yourself. I'm sure I don't want to lug it all the way to the back door. It looks pretty heavy to me.'

The baker went in at the gate and walked up the drive like a little strutting bantam. The children watched him and laughed. 'What a funny little fellow,' said Bets. 'So proud of his clean bread too.

You'd think he would keep his hands clean as well, if he's as clean as all that! They're filthy!'

They watched him disappear round the bend of the drive, looking spruce and smart in his little white coat, breeches, and small-sized, highly-polished boots with polished gaiters above.

'Most disappointing,' he said, as he came back again. 'No thief today anywhere. I don't mind telling you I'm on the lookout now. Anyone suspicious and I tell the police! I promised Mr Goon that. I go into nearly everyone's house, and I'm keeping my eyes open for him. He thinks there'll be more robberies soon!'

'Really?' said Larry politely. The little baker strutted back to his van whistling.

'Very pleased with himself, isn't he?' said Larry. 'I don't think I like him much.'

'Now, let's go down to Frinton Lea and see if we can find Fatty,' said Bets, jumping off the gate.

'Yes, let's,' said Daisy, pleased. 'We've done our bits now – not that we've found out anything.'

They walked down the lane to the river, then along the river-path that led to Frinton Lea. They soon came in sight of it. It was a big, rambling house, once built by rich people, and now owned by someone who ran it for paying guests.

Boats slid by on the water. Fishermen sat by the bank, stolid and patient, almost like bits of the scenery. Each had his little camp-stool, and each hunched himself over his rod, watching his float like a cat watching a mouse-hole.

'I've never seen any of these fishermen catch a fish yet,' said Bets, stopping by one.

'Sh!' said the fisherman angrily, and Bets went away, alarmed.

'You'll frighten away the fish he doesn't catch,' said Pip with a laugh. 'For goodness sake, don't go and disturb a fisherman again!'

They passed two labourers in a field, and then came to Frinton Lea. They looked about expectantly for a heavily disguised Fatty. Was he anywhere about?

At first they could see nobody – and then, sitting in a little boat, not far from the bank, was a hunched-up figure, silently fishing. He had on the most extraordinary clothes.

His hat was a large cloth cap with a rather loud check pattern. His scarf was a curious sickly green. His coat was very tight blue alpaca, and he wore red braces that showed in front where the coat fell open.

The children stared at this peculiar figure. It took one look at them and then glanced away.

'There's *Fatty*!' said Pip. 'But what a get-up! It's not so much a disguise as fancy dress. What's he thinking of to dress like that!'

'He must have some reason for it,' said Daisy. 'Fatty never does anything without a reason. What braces!'

'Did you see his face when he looked round at us?' said Larry with a laugh. 'Fierce eyebrows and a fierce moustache, and he must have got his cheekpads in again, his face looks so fat.'

'I do wish he would look at us properly,' said Bets, who simply couldn't recognise Fatty at all.

'Don't be silly,' said Pip. 'He hopes we won't recognise him, the goof.'

Still the fisherman in the boat didn't look in their direction. He fished stolidly. Then he coughed.

'Very good cough,' said Pip in a loud voice. The fisherman took no notice.

'Pssssssst!' Larry said to him, and still he didn't

so much as turn his head. Any ordinary fisherman would certainly have lost his temper by now and ordered them away. It was most definitely Fatty.

'Don't be goofy!' called Pip in a low voice.

'We've spotted you!' said Daisy, also keeping her voice low. 'It was easy!'

The fisherman obstinately refused to look in their direction. After a little more 'Psssssssting' and attempts to make him turn round, the four gave up.

'We'll walk home and come back afterwards,' said Larry. 'It's getting late.'

They walked home, had their lunches, and came back again. Perhaps Fatty would be more amenable this afternoon.

'The boat's gone,' said Daisy. 'Oh no – look, it's there by the bank. And the fisherman is sitting on the grass, eating his lunch. *Now* we can get him to talk!'

They went up to him and sat down solemnly. He took a hurried look at them and then swallowed a mouthful so quickly that he choked.

'Bad luck,' said Larry, sympathetically. 'Caught many fish?'

'No,' said the fisherman in a strangled sort of

voice. He got up suddenly and went to his boat.

'Pssst!' said Larry. The fisherman clambered hurriedly into his boat, making it rock up and down. Larry was about to go to his help, meaning to whisper a few stinging remarks into Fatty's ear, when Bets caught hold of him and pulled him back. He looked down at her in surprise.

She looked up at him and shook her head, her eyes wide and frightened. She nodded towards the fisherman's boots. They were enormous – and so were his hairy hands!

Larry stopped with a jerk. Gosh – it wasn't Fatty after all! Of course it wasn't. Who was it then? And why had he behaved so strangely?

'Big feet – enormous hands!' whispered Bets. 'It's the thief! It is, Larry – it must be! That's why he's tried to shake us off. He's afraid we're on his track.'

The fisherman had pushed off into the river again. He sat now with his back to the children, hunched up as before. They gazed at him silently. How could they possibly have thought he was Fatty?

'What are we to do?' asked Daisy in a low voice. 'We ought to tell Fatty. But where is he? Is he somewhere near – in disguise? We can't let the thief go now we've found him! Where *is* Fatty? I simply can't see him anywhere!'

10. TELEPHONE CALL TO GOON

Larry thought hard. He was the head of the five when Fatty was not there. What was the best thing to do?

'If only we could spot Fatty!' he groaned. 'I'll tell you what we'd better do. Pip, you and Bets stay here and keep an eye on the thief. Daisy and I will wander about a bit and see if we can spot Fatty. He said he'd be within fifty yards of Frinton Lea, so he will be.'

'Right,' said Pip, and he and Bets settled down on the grassy bank. The other two walked off down the path. The fisherman heard their footsteps and turned round cautiously to see who it was.

'See him look round?' whispered Bets. 'He hoped we'd gone! Then I bet he was going to row to the shore and escape.'

It was rather dull sitting and watching the

fisherman. He didn't catch a single fish. He just sat there with his rod, seemingly asleep.

But he wasn't. He suddenly gave a nasty hollow cough. Bets clutched Pip.

'Did you hear that? I'm sure it's the thief now. He coughed just like a sheep barking – just like Mrs Williams said he did. I wish he'd do it again.'

He didn't. He slumped back in the boat and appeared to be asleep. But he wasn't, because whenever anyone came by, he turned and gave a quick look.

Not many people came by, however. The postman cycled by with some letters. The telegraph boy came once, whistling loudly as he turned in at Frinton Lea. The fisherman turned to give him a quick look, and the children eyed him well too, wondering if he could possibly be Fatty. But he wasn't. He was too thin.

A nanny came by with a pram, and then the little baker appeared with his basket of bread. He had had to leave his van a good way away because there was no road right down to the river, only a path.

He recognised Pip and Bets, as he walked up

with his cocky little stride. 'Hello, hello, *hello*!' he said in his high, sparrow-like voice. 'Here we are again! How many loaves today? Caught any thieves yet?'

Pip thought it was silly of the baker to talk to him as if he was about six years old. He merely jerked his head at him and turned away. But the baker was not to be put off.

He came up and gazed at the fisherman in the boat. 'There's a nice easy job!' he chattered on. 'Sitting in the sun with water lapping all round you, having a nap away from everyone else. Nobody to disturb you. No heavy basket to carry. My, why aren't I a fisherman?'

The fisherman had already turned his head once to glance at the baker. Now he took no notice. The baker called out to him.

'Hey there! Caught any fish?'

The fisherman did not turn round. 'Not yet!' he said in a curious deep voice.

The baker stood and talked away to Pip and Bets, but they took as little notice of him as the fisherman. They thought he was silly. He went at last, carrying his basket of bread through the gate of Frinton Lea.

'Silly little idiot,' said Pip. 'He's too big for his boots. He's got such a high opinion of himself that he just can't see he's a nuisance.'

'Well, let's move a little way off till he comes out again and goes,' said Bets, so they got up and walked in the opposite direction. The baker soon came out, gave them a wave, and strutted off on his spindly legs to his van.

'I wonder how Larry and Daisy are getting on,' said Bets. 'I hope they've found Fatty. It's maddening not to have him just at this important moment.'

Larry and Daisy had wandered all round Frinton Lea, but they hadn't seen Fatty. They had felt sure they had got him once – when they had seen a woman sitting on a stool, painting a picture of the river. She was rather big and had untidy hair and a hat that hid her face. Daisy nudged Larry.

'That's Fatty, surely! See – that woman painting. It would be a fine way of sitting and watching a house – to pretend to be an artist.'

'Yes. It might be Fatty,' said Larry. 'We'll stroll over and see.'

The woman looked up at them as they came and stood beside her. At once Daisy and Larry knew she was not Fatty. Her nose was far too small. Fatty could make his nose bigger – but he certainly couldn't make it smaller!

'No go!' said Larry gloomily. 'Where on earth is he?'

'He might be one of those fishermen,' said Daisy. 'Look – sitting solemnly fishing on the bank. That one over there looks most like Fatty – the way he's sitting somehow. And he's got a position that gives him a very good view of Frinton Lea.'

'That's the one who said "Sh" to Bets,' said Larry. 'We'd better be careful, or he'll shush us too. Walk up very very quietly.'

So they walked up softly – so softly that the fisherman didn't hear them coming at all. They looked at his hands – hands were always a giveaway, because they couldn't very well be altered. But the fisherman wore gloves. They looked at his feet – he wore Wellingtons! He also wore a large shady hat that hid his face.

The fisherman had no idea at all that anyone was just behind him. He suddenly opened his mouth and gave a bored yawn – and that gave the game away at once! It was Fatty's yawn! Fatty always yawned loud and long, and this was Fatty all right.

Larry sat down beside him with Daisy on the other side. 'Fatty!' said Larry in a low voice. 'We've found the thief.'

The fisherman immediately became Fatty, and gave a low whistle. He looked down at Larry and Larry felt quite startled. The eyes were Fatty's, but that was all! Fatty had his false teeth in, the ones that slid over his own, and he had also done something peculiar to his eyebrows. He wore a silly little moustache, and these things made him look a different person altogether. But his eyes were the same, direct and clear and shrewd.

'What did you say?' asked the fisherman, in Fatty's own voice. Larry repeated what he had said.

'See that fellow over there in the boat?' said Larry. 'Well, he's the thief! You should see his enormous feet and hands – and he's got a cough like a sheep too. He's the one, Fatty. I bet he lives at Frinton Lea. We've found him!'

Fatty was silent for a moment. 'Are you sure

about it?' he said at last. 'Well, I'll sit here and keep an eye on him and you go and telephone Mr Goon.'

'Telephone Mr *Goon*?' said Larry, surprised. 'Why should we let *him* know? We're not working with *him*, are we?'

'Do as I say,' said Fatty. 'If he's not in, telephone again after a while. Tell him all about the awful fellow in the boat. He'll be thrilled. Tell him I'm keeping an eye on him till he comes down to arrest him.'

Larry and Daisy were puzzled. They looked at Fatty, but his face was so different, with its protruding teeth and moustache and eyebrows, that they could not tell what he was really thinking.

'All right,' said Larry, getting up, puzzled that Fatty did not show more excitement. He went off with Daisy to find Bets and Pip.

'I believe old Fatty's quite jealous because we found the thief before he did,' said Larry. 'Pretty tame ending to the mystery anyway – handing the thief over to Mr Goon like this!'

Daisy was disappointed too. It wasn't like Fatty to be jealous. They went to Bets and Pip and sat down beside them. They told them in a whisper what they were to do.

'We'll *all* go and telephone,' said Daisy. 'I'm fed up with messing about here now. Fatty says he'll keep an eye on the thief out there. He can see him from where he is.'

They left the river and walked back up to the town. They decided to go to the post office to telephone – but, alas, Mr Goon was not in. His cleaning lady answered the phone. She didn't know where he was, but said he had left a note to say he would be back by half past four at the latest.

'Blow! It's only about a quarter *to* four now,' said Larry. 'Let's go and get some ice cream and lemonade, and wait for a bit.'

So they had ice creams – two each – and iced lemonade in the little sweetshop. That took them about half an hour. Then they strolled back to the telephone box to try their luck again.

This time, Mr Goon answered the telephone himself. Larry looked round at the others. 'He's in,' he said. 'Good!'

'Police here,' said Goon's voice sounding gruff and sharp. 'What is it?'

'Mr Goon! It's Laurence speaking, Frederick Trotteville's friend,' said Larry. 'I've something to report – about that robbery case – the two cases, I mean.'

'Well – go on,' said Goon sharply.

'We've found the thief,' said Larry, unable to keep the excitement out of his voice. 'We saw him today.'

'Where?' asked Mr Goon.

'In a boat just opposite Frinton Lea,' said Larry. 'He's been there ages. Probably he lives at the boarding-house. You remember there was a scrap of paper with Frinton on it?'

There was a peculiar noise at the other end. 'What did you say?' said Larry, but Mr Goon was silent. Larry went on eagerly.

'He's a frightful-looking fellow, Mr Goon. We recognised him because of his colossal feet and huge hands. He's very ugly – puffy cheeks, rather protruding eyes – and he's got a cough like a sheep – just like Mrs Williams and Jinny said. If you go down to the river now, you'll catch him. Fatty's keeping his eye on him for you.'

Larry paused. Goon didn't seem to be taking

this in. 'Mr Goon – are you going to arrest him?' asked Larry.

A loud snort came down the telephone – then a bang. Goon had put down his receiver so hard that surely he must have chipped it!

'He's rung off,' said Larry amazed. 'Whatever's the matter with him?'

11. A TEA PARTY - AND A BRAINWAVE

Larry and the others stepped out of the telephone box into which they had all crowded. Larry repeated the conversation. They were all very puzzled.

'Better go back and tell Fatty,' said Larry at last. 'It's quite obvious that Mr Goon doesn't believe us. So *we* shall have to do something about it now. I've a good mind to ring the Inspector.'

'No. Don't do that till we've asked Fatty,' said Bets. 'It seems to me there's something funny about all this. Let's go back to Fatty.'

'Why – there he is!' said Daisy suddenly, and sure enough, there *was* Fatty! He was himself now, very spruce and clean, with Buster trotting delightedly at his heels.

The others poured out of the post office and stared in astonishment at Fatty, who grinned back.

'Fatty! Have you left him? How did you get home and change so quickly? What's happened?' asked Larry.

'Oh, he went immediately after you left,' said Fatty. 'So I left too, of course.'

'Did you follow him? Where did he go?' asked Daisy.

'No. I didn't follow him,' said Fatty. 'There wasn't any point in doing so – I knew quite well where he was going. Did you telephone Mr Goon?'

'Yes. He was out the first time – but we got him the second time,' said Larry. 'I told him all about the frightful fellow in the boat – all the details, of course – and he just gave a snort and banged the receiver down. I suppose he didn't believe me.'

Fatty suddenly began to laugh. He laughed as if he had been keeping it in for some time. He exploded, held on to the railings, and laughed till the tears came into his eyes. Bets began to laugh too. He looked so funny, and his laughter was really infectious.

'What's the *matter*?' said Larry suspiciously. 'What's the joke? You're acting most peculiarly today, Fatty. So is Mr Goon.'

'Yes. You're right about *him*,' said Fatty, wiping his eyes. 'Oh dear – I'd have given anything to see Mr Goon's face when you rang him up and told him what a hideous fellow he was, with his big feet and hands and protruding eyes!'

The others stared, puzzled at first – and then a great light dawned on them. Larry sank down on to a wooden bench by the bus stop. He felt suddenly weak.

'Gosh! You don't mean to say – you don't *really* mean to say that that frightful fisherman in the boat was Mr *Goon* – Mr Goon himself!'

'Well – think back to him,' said Fatty. 'How you could all fall for that ridiculous disguise of his, I really don't know. You ought to be ashamed of yourselves. Why, Mr Goon himself stuck out a mile in that frightful get-up. And you actually go and think he's the thief!'

'Oh, Fatty – *I* put the idea into the others' heads,' said Bets, as if she was going to burst into tears. 'I saw his big feet – and hands – oh, Fatty!'

'You beast, Fatty – you told us to go and telephone Mr Goon – and we've gone and described him to himself!' said Daisy, full of horror.

'Oh, Fatty – you really are a beast.'

'Serves you right,' said Fatty unfeelingly, and began to laugh again. 'Fine lot of detectives you are, I must say – go and hunt for a thief and pick on the only policeman of the village, in disguise! As Mr Goon would say – Gah!'

'No wonder he snorted and banged the receiver down,' said Daisy, still more alarmed. 'I hope he won't go round and complain to our parents again.'

'He won't,' said Fatty. 'He doesn't know whether you really fell for his disguise or not. If he thinks you did, he'll be very happy to think he took you in. If he thinks you saw through his disguise and were pulling his leg when you phoned, he'll feel a bit of an idiot. He won't say a word either way. He'll only snort.'

'He won't be very fond of us now,' said Pip.

'He never was,' said Fatty. 'All the same, I was surprised to see him there this morning. I spotted him at once out in that boat.'

'You would!' said Larry, half-annoyed and half-admiring.

'When I saw him I knew he'd had the same idea as we had about Frinton Lea,' said Fatty.

'And what's more, he'll probably go and snoop outside Rods now, wherever that is.'

'Do you think it's much good snooping round either Frinton Lea or Rods, wherever that is?' asked Larry.

'No, I don't think I do,' said Fatty, considering the point. 'It's just that we can't afford to leave any clue unexplored. If we do, it's bound to be the only one that might lead us to the solution! Anyway, I had a bit of luck this afternoon, just before you came to talk to me, Larry and Daisy.'

'What?' asked Larry. 'You're a lucky beggar, Fatty – you always have any bit of luck that's going.'

'I was sitting fishing, when that artist woman came by,' said Fatty. 'I expect you saw her. My hat blew off at that very moment and she picked it up for me. I began to talk to her – and it turned out that she lives at Frinton Lea!'

'Golly!' said Larry. 'So you asked a few leading questions, I suppose?'

Fatty grinned. 'I did! And I found out that the only man staying at Frinton Lea has been very ill and is only just allowed to get up. So we can rule him out as the thief, who must be an agile fellow, to say the least of it!'

'Oh – well, that's good,' said Daisy. 'Your day hasn't been wasted, Fatty. You didn't see the thief, but you did find out he wasn't at Frinton Lea.'

'Your day wasn't wasted either,' said Fatty, beginning to laugh again. 'I hope I don't think of you telephoning old Mr Goon when I'm having dinner with my parents tonight. I shall choke if I do.'

'What about tea?' said Bets. 'I'm getting hungry.'

'You've just had two ice creams and a lemonade!' said Pip.

'Well, they don't make any difference,' said Bets. 'You don't eat those, you just swallow them. Anyway, we'd better go home quickly or we'll be too late for tea.'

'I'll treat you all,' said Fatty generously. 'I've got enough money on me.' He pulled out a handful of change and examined it. 'Yes, come on. We'll go to Oliver's and have meringues and chocolate slices – in celebration of finding the thief-who-wasn't.'

Everyone laughed. Bets took Fatty's arm. Dear, generous Fatty – he always seemed to have plenty of money, but he always shared it round. Bets squeezed his arm affectionately.

'The mystery's getting on, isn't it?' she said. 'We've ruled out Frinton Lea. Now we've got to find out what "1 Rods" is, and rule that out too.'

'Well, we won't be much further on with the mystery, silly, if we keep examining our clues and finding they're no good,' said Pip, exasperated with his small sister. 'Anyway, "1 Rods" sounds more like a note made by someone going fishing than anything else.'

'It's an idea,' said Fatty, taking them all into Oliver's. They sat down and ordered lemonade, egg sandwiches, meringues, chocolate éclairs and chocolate slices. Bets' mouth began to water.

'I never know whether to eat as quickly as possible so as to enjoy everything before I stop feeling hungry, or to eat slowly and taste every single bit,' said Bets, eyeing the pile of delicious-looking cakes.

'Don't be silly,' said Pip scornfully. 'You stop feeling hungry as soon as you've eaten a certain amount, whether you've eaten it quickly or not.'

'You eat how you like, Bets,' said Fatty, who always stuck up for Bets when her brother ticked her off. They all began on their tea, having a friendly argument as to whether the meringues were better than the éclairs. The dish was soon empty and Fatty, after examining his money again, called for a fresh supply.

'About this Rods place,' said Fatty. 'It's either the name of a house, shortened – or else it's the name of a family, either complete or shortened. I've never heard of anyone called Rods though.'

'How could we find out?' wondered Larry. 'We could look in the telephone book for names beginning with Rod or Rods.'

'Yes, that's a good idea,' said Daisy, taking her second éclair. 'And we've got a street directory at home, with everyone's house in it, and the name or number.'

'You're talking good sense,' said Fatty, sounding pleased. 'Anyone got an idea for finding a person with enormous feet? Apart from examining the feet of everyone we meet, I mean. I've rather ruled that out – it would be frightful to look at nothing but feet, feet, feet, all day long wherever we go.'

Bets giggled. 'And even if we find someone with

colossal feet, we can't very well stop them and say, "Excuse me, may I see the pattern of the rubber heels you're wearing?" '

'No, we can't,' said Pip. 'But I say – I tell you what we *could* do – I've just thought of it. It's a brainwave!'

'What?' asked everyone together.

Pip dropped his voice. One or two people in the shop seemed rather too interested in what they were all saying, he thought.

'Why can't we go to the cobbler's – there *is* only one in Peterswood now the other man's gone – and ask if he ever has any size twelve boots in for repair and, if so, whose are they?'

There was a little silence after this remarkable suggestion. Then Fatty solemnly reached out and shook hands with Pip.

'First class!' he said. 'Brilliant! Talk about a brainwave! Go up top, Pip. That really *may* lead us somewhere!'

12. FATTY,
THE COBBLER - AND GOON

The next day, they set to work to follow up the suggestions made at the tea shop. Daisy and Larry said they would look up the streets directory and read down every single street to see if there was a house name beginning with Rod or Rods.

Pip and Bets were to look in the telephone directory for names. Fatty was to go to the cobbler's. Nobody particularly wanted to do that, because they couldn't think how to go about it without making the cobbler think they were either mad or silly.

'I'll manage it,' said Fatty. 'I'll think of a way. And, for goodness sake, don't get taken in again by any disguise of Mr Goon's – he's been studying hard, I can see, on his refresher course, and goodness knows what he'll produce next.'

'I shall just look at his feet,' said Bets, 'and

if they're enormous, I'll know they belong to Mr Goon!'

Fatty considered carefully how to approach the cobbler. He was known to be a hot-tempered man who would stand no nonsense at all. He would have to go to him with a sensible idea of some sort. But what?

Fatty remembered an old second-hand shop he had once seen in Sheepridge. He tried to remember if they sold boots. Yes, he had an idea that they did. In that case, it would be a good idea to catch the bus to Sheepridge, look in the second-hand shop and buy the biggest pair there – they would presumably want mending, and he could take them to the cobbler. Fatty felt certain that with that opening he could soon find out if the cobbler had any customers with really enormous feet.

Then I'll get their names, and see if any of them might be the thief, he thought. So off he went to catch the bus to Sheepridge. He found the second-hand shop and, feeling as if he wanted to hold his nose because of the musty, dusty smell, he went inside.

There was a special box of boots and shoes. Fatty turned them all over, and at the bottom he found what he wanted – a pair of elevens, down at heel, and with a slit in one side.

He bought them very cheaply and went off with them, feeling pleased. He caught the bus back to Peterswood and went home. He debated whether or not to disguise himself, and then decided that he would, just for practice.

He went down to his shed and looked round at his things. An old tramp? He was rather good at that. Yes – that wouldn't be a bad idea at all – he could wear the frightful old boots too! They would make him limp but what did that matter? It would look all the more natural.

Fatty began to work deftly and quickly. He hoped his mother wouldn't come and look for him. She would be scared to see a dirty old tramp in the shed. After about half an hour the door opened, and the tramp came out and peered round cautiously.

He looked dreadful. Fatty had blacked out two of his front teeth, and had put in one cheekpad so that it looked as if he had toothache on the right side of his face. He had put on grey, untrimmed eyebrows, and had stuck on a bristly little grey moustache. His face was lined with dirty creases and wrinkles. Fatty was adept at creasing up his face! His wig was one of his best – grey straggling hair with a bald patch in the middle.

Fatty had laughed at himself when he looked in the long glass he kept in his shed. What a tramp! He wore holey old gloves on his hands, dirty corduroy trousers, an equally dirty shirt – and the boots!

Fatty could only hobble along in them, so he took an ash-stick he had cut from the hedge on one of his walks to help him along. He stuck an old clay pipe in the corner of his mouth and grinned at himself. He felt really proud, and for half-a-minute wondered if he should present himself at the back door and ask for a crust of bread from the cook.

He decided not to. The last time he had done that the cook had screamed the place down, and his mother had very nearly caught him. He went cautiously out of the shed to the gate at the bottom of the garden. He was not going to risk meeting any of his household.

The old tramp hobbled down the road, sucking at his empty pipe, and making funny little grunting noises. He made his way to the cobbler's and went inside the dark little shop.

The cobbler was at the back, working. He came into the shop when the bell rang. 'What do you want?' he said.

'Oooh – ah,' said Fatty, taking his pipe out of his mouth. 'It's my boots, Mister. They hurt me something crool. Too small they are, and they want mending too. You got any bigger ones to sell?'

The cobbler bent over his counter to look at Fatty's feet. 'What size are they – elevens or twelves?' he said. 'No, I haven't got that size to sell. It's a big size.'

The old tramp gave a peculiar wheezy laugh. 'Ah yes, it's big. I was a big man once, I was! I bet you haven't got anyone in this here neighbourhood that's got feet bigger than mine!'

'There's two people with big feet here,' said the cobbler, considering. 'There's Mr Goon the policeman and there's Colonel Cross – they're the biggest of all. I charge them more when I sole their boots – the leather I use for their repairs! Do you want me to mend your boots?'

'Ay, I do – if you can get me another pair to put on while you mend these,' said the old tramp, and he gave his wheezy laugh again. 'Or couldn't I borrow a pair of Colonel Cross's – have you got a pair in to mend?'

'No, I haven't – and you wouldn't get 'em if I had,' said the cobbler sharply. 'Get along with you! Do you want to get me into trouble?'

'No, no,' said the old tramp. 'Do his boots have rubber heels on?'

The cobbler lost his temper. 'What's that to do with you? Coming in here wasting my time! You'll be wanting to know if the butcher has brown or black laces next. Be off with you, and don't come back again.'

'That's all right, sir, that's all right,' wheezed the old man, shuffling to the door, where he stopped and had a most alarming coughing fit.

'You stop smoking a clay pipe and you'll get rid of that cough,' said the cobbler, bad-temperedly. Then he saw someone else trying to get past the coughing tramp. 'Get out of my shop and let the next person come in.'

The next person was a burly man with a little black moustache, a dark brown face, dark glasses, and big feet.

He pushed past the old tramp. 'Give me room,' he said in a sharp voice. Fatty pricked up his ears at once. He knew that familiar voice – yes, and he knew that unfamiliar figure too – it was Mr Goon!

Goon! In *another* disguise! thought Fatty in amazement and mirth. He's done better this time – with dark glasses to hide his frog-eyes, and some stuff on his red face to make it look tanned.

He looked at the burly Goon. He wore white flannel trousers and a shirt with no tie, and a red belt round his portly middle. On his feet were enormous white shoes.

Why the disguise? wondered Fatty. Just practising, like me? Or is he going to snoop round somewhere? Perhaps he has found out where or who Rods is. I'd better stand by and find out.

He shuffled out and sat down on a wooden bench, just outside. He strained his ears to see if he could catch any words. What was Goon doing in the cobbler's? Surely he hadn't got the same bright idea as Pip had had – of asking about repairs to large-size boots!

Goon had! He was very pleased about it. He had made up a nice little story to help him along.

'Good morning,' he said to the cobbler. 'Did my brother leave his boots here to be mended? He asked me to come in and see. Very large size, twelves or thirteens.'

'What name?' asked the cobbler.

'He didn't give his name,' said Mr Goon. 'Just left the boots, he said.'

'Well, I haven't any boots as big as that here,' said the cobbler. 'I've only got two customers with feet that size.'

'Who are they?' asked Goon.

'What's that to you?' said the cobbler impatiently. 'Am I going to waste all my morning talking about big boots?'

'I know one of your customers is Mr Goon,' said Mr Goon. 'I know Mr Goon very well. He's a great friend of mine. Very nice fellow.'

'Oh, *is* he? Then you know him better than I do,' said the cobbler. 'I've got no time for that pompous old policeman.'

Mr Goon went purple under his tan. 'Who's your other customer?' he asked, in such an unexpectedly fierce voice that the cobbler stared. 'The one with big feet, I mean. You'd better answer my question. For all you know, I might have been sent here by Mr Goon himself!'

'Bah!' said the cobbler, and then thought better of it. 'The other fellow is Colonel Cross,' he said.

'Does he have rubber heels?' asked Mr Goon and was immediately amazed by the cobbler's fury.

'Rubber heels! How many more people want to know if he has rubber heels! What do I care? Go and ask him yourself!' raged the cobbler, going as purple as Mr Goon. 'You and that old tramp are a pair, you are!'

'What old tramp?' asked Goon in surprise.

'The one you pushed past at the door – with feet as big as yourself!' raged the cobbler. 'Clear out of my shop now. I've got work to do. Rubber heels!'

Goon went out with great dignity. He longed to tell the cobbler who he was – what a shock for him that would be. What was it he had called him? 'A pompous old policeman!' Goon put that away in his memory. One day he would make the cobbler sorry for that rude remark!

Now, what about this tramp with big feet? Where was he? He might be the thief! There didn't seem many people with enormous feet in

Peterswood as far as he could find out – only himself and Colonel Cross. He would have to enquire about Colonel Cross's boots – see if they had rubber heels – though it wasn't very likely that Colonel Cross went burgling other people's houses.

Goon blinked in the bright sunshine, quite glad of his dark glasses. Where was that tramp? Well – what a piece of luck – there he was, sitting on the bench nearby!

Goon sat down heavily beside him. Fatty took one look and longed to laugh. He saw Mr Goon looking at his big old boots. Ah – they had roused his suspicions. Well, Fatty was quite prepared to sit there as long as Goon – and to have a bit of fun too. He stuck his boots out well in front of him. Come on, Mr Goon – say something!

13. A LITTLE BIT OF FUN

Goon hadn't the slightest idea that he was sitting next to Fatty. He looked through his dark glasses at the old man. Could he be the thief? He tried to see his hands, but Fatty was still wearing the holey old gloves.

'Want some baccy?' said Mr Goon, seeing that Fatty's clay pipe was empty.

Fatty looked at him and then put his hand behind his ear.

'Want some baccy?' said Goon, a little more loudly.

Still Fatty held his hand behind his ear and looked enquiringly at Goon, sucking at his dirty old pipe, and squinting horribly.

'WANT SOME BACCY?' roared Goon.

'Oh, ah – yes – I've got a bad backache,' answered Fatty. 'Oooh, my backache. Something crool, it is.'

'I said, "WANT SOME BACCY?" ' yelled Goon again.

'I heard you the first time,' said Fatty, with dignity. 'I'm having treatment for it at the hospital. And for me pore old feet too.'

He gave a long, wheezy cough and rubbed the back of his hand over his nose.

'You've got big feet!' said Goon loudly.

'Oh, ah – it's a nice sunny seat,' agreed the old tramp. 'I allus sits here of a mornin'.'

'I said – "you've got BIG FEET," ' shouted Goon.

'You're right. Not enough meat these days,' said the tramp and coughed again. ' 'Taint right. Meat's good for you.'

Goon gave it up. 'Silly old man,' he said in his ordinary voice, thinking that the tramp was absolutely stone deaf. Most surprisingly, the old fellow heard him.

'Here! Who are you calling a silly old man?' said the tramp fiercely. 'I heard you! Yes, I did! Think I was deaf, did you? But I heard you!'

'Now now – don't be silly,' said Goon, alarmed at the disturbance the tramp was making. 'Be calm.'

'Harm! Yes, I'll harm you!' said the tramp, and

actually raised his stick. Goon retreated hurriedly to the other end of the bench and debated with himself. This old chap couldn't be the thief. He was deaf, his feet were bad, and he had backache. But where had he got those boots? It might be as well to follow him home and find out where he lived. It was no good asking him, that was plain. He'd only make some silly reply. So Goon took out his own pipe and proceeded to fill it, and to wait until the old tramp moved off.

Fatty was also waiting for Goon to move off, because he wanted to see if the policeman had discovered who or where Rods was. So there they both sat, one sucking an empty pipe, the other preparing and filling one.

And then he saw Larry, Daisy, Bets and Pip coming down the street! Thank goodness they hadn't got Buster, who would certainly have smelt Fatty at once and greeted him with joy. Buster was safely locked up in the shed, and was no doubt still scraping hopefully at the door.

Fatty sank his chin down on his chest, hoping that none of the four would recognise him. It would be maddening if they did, and came over to him and gave the game away to Goon.

They didn't recognise him. They gave him a mere glance, and then rested their eyes on Goon.

They walked by, giving backward glances at the disguised policeman, who pulled at his pipe desperately, praying that the four would go away. Thank goodness that big boy was not with them. He'd have spotted him at once, disguise or no disguise.

The four children stopped at the end of the street because Bets was pulling at Larry's sleeve so urgently. 'What is it, Bets?' asked Larry.

'See that big man sitting on the bench by the dirty old tramp?' said Bets. 'I'm sure it's Mr Goon! I'd know his big hairy hands anywhere. He's in disguise again – a better disguise this time, because his eyes are hidden. You just simply can't mistake those when you see them.'

'I believe Bets is right,' said Daisy, looking back. 'Yes – you can see it's Mr Goon – the way he sits, and everything. It *is* Mr Goon!'

'Let's have a bit of fun with him then,' said Pip. 'Come on, let's. He won't know if we've spotted him or not, and he'll be in an awful fix.'

Bets giggled. 'What shall we do?'

'Oh nothing much – just go up to him innocently and ask him questions,' said Larry. 'You know – what's the time, please? Have you got any change? Where does the bus start?'

Everyone laughed. 'I'll go first,' said Pip. He walked up to the bench. Fatty saw him coming, and felt alarmed. Surely Pip hadn't recognised him. It looked as if he was going to speak to him. No – Pip was talking to Mr Goon!

'Could you please tell me the time?' Pip asked innocently. Mr Goon scowled. He pulled out his big watch.

'Ten to twelve,' he said.

'Thanks very much,' said Pip. Fatty was astonished. Pip had his own watch. What was the point? Gosh! – could the others have recognised Mr Goon after all – and have made up their minds to have some fun with him?

Larry came next. 'Oh – could you possibly give me some change, sir?' he asked Goon politely. Fatty almost choked, but his choke was lost in Goon's snort.

'No. Clear orf,' said Mr Goon, unable to stop

himself from using his favourite expression.

'Thanks very much,' said Larry politely and went off. Fatty got out his handkerchief, ready to bury his face in it if any of the others came along with a request. He hadn't bargained for this.

Up came Daisy. 'Could you tell me, please, if the bus stops here for Sheepridge?' she asked.

Goon nearly exploded. Those kids! Here he was, in a perfectly splendid disguise, one good enough to prevent anyone from knowing him, one that should be absolute protection against these pests of children – and here they all were, making a beeline for him. Did they do this sort of thing to everybody? He'd have to report them – complain to their parents!

'Go and look at the bus timetable,' he snapped at Daisy.

'Oh, thank you very much,' she said. Fatty chortled again into his handkerchief and Daisy looked at him in surprise. What a funny old man.

Bets was the last to come. 'Please, have you seen our little dog, Buster?' she asked.

'No,' roared Goon. 'And if I do, I'll chase him out of town.'

'Oh, thanks very much,' said Bets politely, and departed. Fatty was nearly dying of laughter, trying to keep back his guffaws. He had another coughing fit in his handkerchief and Goon looked at him suspiciously.

'Nasty cough of yours,' he said. Poor Fatty was quite unable to answer. He prayed that the others wouldn't come back to ask any more questions.

Goon was debating with himself again. With those children about, pestering him like this, he'd never get anywhere. Had they seen through his disguise? Or was this kind of thing their usual behaviour? He saw Daisy bearing down on him and rose hurriedly. He strode off in the direction of the police station. He could bear no more.

Fatty collapsed. He buried his face in his handkerchief and laughed till he cried. Daisy looked at him in alarm. 'Are you all right?' she said timidly.

Fatty recovered and sat up. 'Yes thanks, Daisy,' he said in his normal voice, and Daisy stood and stared at him, her mouth open in amazement.

'Fatty!' she whispered. 'Oh, *Fatty*! We

recognised Goon – but we didn't know the tramp was you! Oh, Fatty!'

'Listen,' said Fatty. 'I don't want to have to change out of this disguise – it takes ages to take off and put on – and I want to see if Mr Goon has found out anything about Rods. He's using his brains over all this, you know. Thought about going to see the cobbler and everything, just as we did. I don't want him to get ahead of us. I think I'd better trail him today.'

'All right,' said Daisy, sitting down near to him, and speaking in a low voice. 'You want us to get you some lunch, I suppose? There's a bus stop near Mr Goon's house. You could sit there and eat your lunch and read a paper – and watch for Mr Goon at the same time.'

'Yes – that's what I'll do,' said Fatty. 'I feel somehow as if Mr Goon's got going on this. If he's going to get ahead of us, I want to know about it.'

'I couldn't find the streets directory this morning,' said Daisy, talking straight out in front of her, so that nobody would think she was talking to an old tramp. 'Larry's borrowing one this afternoon. Pip found two names in the telephone directory that might help – one is Rodney, the other is Roderick. The Rodneys live up on the hill, and the Rodericks live near you.'

'Oh yes – I remember now,' said Fatty. 'Well, we can rule the Rodericks out, I think. There's only an old lady, a Mrs Roderick, and a young one, a Miss. There's no one there who wears size twelve shoes. I don't know about the Rodneys though.'

'Shall I and the others go and see if we can find out anything at the Rodneys?' said Daisy. 'We could go this afternoon. Mummy knows them, so I could easily go on some excuse.'

'There's a jumble sale on in the town,' said Fatty. 'Couldn't you go and ask for jumble? *Especially* old boots – large size if possible as you know an old tramp who wears them!'

Daisy giggled. 'You do have bright ideas, Fatty,' she said. 'I suppose you're the old tramp who wears them! Yes, I'll go and ask for jumble. Bets can go with me. I'll go over to the others now. They're standing there wondering what on earth I'm doing, talking to myself!'

They were certainly very surprised to see Daisy sitting down after Goon had so hurriedly departed, apparently murmuring away to herself. They were just about to come over when she left the bench and went to them.

'What's up with you?' asked Larry. Daisy smiled delightedly. 'That was Fatty!' she whispered. 'Don't recognise him, for goodness' sake. We've got to get some lunch for him somehow, because he thinks Mr Goon is on the track of something and he wants to trail him.'

The four marched solemnly past Fatty on the bench, and each got a wink from the old tramp.

'We're going off to get lunch,' said Daisy loudly, as if she was speaking to Larry. But the tramp knew quite well that she was speaking to *him*!

14. A VERY BUSY AFTERNOON

Fatty shuffled his way to the bus stop bench near Goon's house. He let himself down slowly as if he indeed had a bad back. He let out a grunt. An old lady on the bench looked at him sympathetically. Poor old man! She leaned across and pressed some money into his hand.

Fatty was so taken aback that he almost forgot he was a tramp. He remembered immediately though, and put his finger to his forehead in exactly the same way that his father's old chauffeur did when he came to see him.

'Thank you kindly,' he wheezed.

There was no sign of Mr Goon. He had gone hurriedly into the back door of his house, and was now engaged in stripping off his disguise. He was going out in his official clothes this afternoon – PC Goon – and woe betide any cobblers or others who were rude to him!

Soon Daisy came slipping back with a picnic lunch, done up in a piece of newspaper. Fatty approved of that touch! Just what he *would* have his lunch in if he really was an old tramp. Good for Daisy! His troop were coming along well, he considered.

Daisy sat down on the bench, bending over to do up her shoe. She spoke to Fatty out of the corner of her mouth. 'Here's your lunch. Best I could get. Larry's looked up the names of houses in the directory he borrowed. There's only one beginning with Rod, and that's one called Rodways, down by Pip's house.'

'Thanks. You go to the Rodneys about the jumble with Bets, and tell Larry and Pip to go to Rodways and snoop,' said Fatty. 'Find out if there's anyone there with large feet, who *might* be the thief. Rodways is only a little cottage, isn't it?'

'Yes,' said Daisy. 'All right. And you're going to trail Goon, aren't you, to see if he's up to something? We'll meet at your shed later.'

She laced up her shoe, sat up, and whispered goodbye. Then off she went – and behind her she left the newspaper of food. Very clever! thought Fatty, opening it. Good old Daisy.

He had a very nice lunch of egg sandwiches, tomato sandwiches and a large slice of fruit cake. Daisy had even slipped in a bottle of ginger beer! Fatty ate and drank everything, and then put his clay pipe back into his mouth again. He opened the newspaper, which was that day's, and began to read very comfortably.

Goon went into his little front room and sat down to go through some papers. He glanced out of the window, and saw the old tramp on the bench.

Turned up again like a bad penny! said Goon to himself. Well, I can certainly keep an eye on him if he sits there. Still, he can't be the thief – he's too doddery.

The tramp read his paper and then apparently fell asleep. Goon had his lunch, did a little telephoning, and then decided to get on with his next job. He looked at his notes.

Frinton Lea. He had crossed that out. What with watching it all day and enquiring about it, he had come to the conclusion that he could forget about that. Now for the other people or places – the

Rodericks – the Rodneys – and that house down the lane – what was it called? – Rodways. One of them must be the Rods on this scrap of paper. 'Rods. It's some sort of clue, that's certain. Good thing those children don't know about these bits of paper. Ha, I'm one up on them there.'

Poor Mr Goon didn't know that PC Tonks had shown them to Fatty, or he wouldn't have been nearly so pleased! He put his papers together, frowned, thought of his plan of campaign, and got up heavily, his great boots clomping loudly as he went out into the hall.

The old tramp was still on the bench. Lazy old thing! thought Mr Goon. He wheeled his bicycle quickly to the front, got on it and sailed away before Fatty could even have time to sit up!

'Blow!' said Fatty. 'He's out of disguise – and on his bike. I'm stuck! I never thought of his bike. I can't trail him on that.'

He wondered what to do. Well, the others were taking care of the Rodneys and the house called Rodways. He'd better go and find Colonel Cross's house. As he was apparently the only other person in Peterswood who wore size twelve or thirteen shoes, he certainly must be enquired into!

Goon had shot off to the Roderick's first. There he found out what Fatty already knew – that there was no man in the house at all. Right. He could cross that off.

He then went to see the Rodneys – and the very first thing he saw there were two bicycles outside the front fence – girls' bicycles, with Daisy and Bets just coming out of the gate towards them!

Those kids again! What were they doing *here*? And whatever were they carrying? Goon glared at them.

'Good afternoon, Mr Goon,' said Daisy, cheerfully. 'Want to come and buy a pair of shoes at the jumble sale?'

Goon eyed the four or five old pairs of boots and shoes wrathfully. 'Where did you get those?' he said.

'From Mrs Rodney,' answered Daisy. 'We're collecting for the jumble sale, Mr Goon. Have *you* got anything that would do for it? An old pair of big boots, perhaps?'

'Mrs Rodney let us look all through her cupboard of boots,' said Bets, 'and she gave us these.'

Goon had nothing to say. He simply stood and glared. The Rodneys! So these pests of kids had got on to that clue too – they were rounding up the Rods just as he was – but they were just one move in front of him.

He debated whether to go in or not now. Mrs Rodney might not welcome somebody else enquiring after shoes. He cast his eye again on the collection of old boots and shoes that Daisy and Bets were stuffing into their bicycle baskets.

Daisy saw his interest in them. 'No. None size twelve,' she said with a giggle. 'Size ten is the very largest the Rodneys have. That will save you a lot of trouble, won't it, Mr Goon?'

'Gah!' said Mr Goon, and leapt angrily on his bicycle. Interfering lot! And how did they know about the Rods anyway? Had Tonks shown those scraps of paper? He'd bite Tonks' head off, if he had!

He rode off to Rodways, the cottage down the lane that led to the river. He was just putting his bicycle against the little wall when he noticed two more there – boys' bicycles this time. Well, if it was any of those little pests' bikes, he'd have something to say!

Larry and Pip were there. They had stopped outside the cottage, apparently to have a game of ball – and one of them had thrown the ball into the cottage garden.

'Careless idiot!' Pip shouted loudly to Larry. 'Now we'll have to go and ask permission to get the ball!'

They went in and knocked at the door, which was wide open. An old woman, sitting in a rocking-chair, peered at them from a corner of the room inside.

'What do you want?' she asked, in a cracked old voice.

'We're so sorry,' said Larry politely. 'Our ball went into your garden. May we get it?'

'Yes,' said the old woman, beginning to rock herself. 'And just tell me if the milkman's been, will you? If he has, the milk bottle will be outside. And did you see the baker down the lane?'

'No, we didn't,' said Pip. 'There *is* a bottle out here on the step. Shall I bring it in?'

'Yes, thank you kindly,' said the old woman. 'Put it in the larder, there's a good lad. That baker!

He gets later every day! I hope I haven't missed him. I fall asleep, you know. I might not have heard him.'

Larry looked round the little cottage. He saw a big sou'wester hanging on a nail, and an enormous oilskin below it. Aha! Somebody big lived here, that was certain.

'What a big oilskin!' he said to the old woman. 'Giant-size!'

'Ah, that's my son's,' said the old woman, rocking away hard. 'He's a big man, he is – but kind and gentle – just like a big dog, I always say.'

Pip had pricked up his ears too, by this time. 'He must be enormous,' he said. 'Whatever size shoes does he wear? Sixteens!'

The old lady gave a cackle of laughter. 'Go on with you! Sixteens! Look over there, on that shelf – those are my son's boots – there's a surprise for you!'

It *was* a surprise – for the shoes were no more than size sevens, about Larry's own size! The boys looked at them in astonishment.

'Does he really only wear size seven?' said Larry. 'What small feet he has for such a big man.'

'Yes. Small feet and small hands – that's what my family always have,' said the old woman, showing her own misshapen but small feet and hands. Pip looked at Larry. Rodways was definitely ruled out. The thief didn't live here!

Someone came up the path and called in. 'Granma! Baker-boy here!'

'Gosh – it's that awful little peacock of a baker again!' said Pip, in disgust. 'We can't seem to get rid of him.'

'One loaf as usual, baker!' called the old lady. 'Put it in my pan for me.'

The baker put down his basket, took a loaf, and strutted in. He saw the two boys, and smiled amiably. 'Here we are again! Come to see old Granma?'

He flung the bread into the pan in the larder and strutted out again. He picked up his basket and went off, whistling, turning out his feet like a duck.

'Now you go and look for your ball,' said the old woman, settling herself comfortably! 'I can go to sleep now I know the milk and the bread have come.'

They went out, found their ball, and Larry threw

it out into the road. There was an angry shout.

'Now then, you there! What are you doing, throwing your ball at me?'

Mr Goon's angry red face appeared over the hedge. The boys gaped in surprise. 'Golly – did it hit you, Mr Goon?' said Pip, with much concern. 'We didn't know you were there.'

'Now look here – what are you *here* for?' demanded Mr Goon. 'Everywhere I go, you're there before me. What are you playing at?'

'Ball,' said Larry, picking up the ball and aiming it at Pip. It missed him, struck the wall, bounced back, and struck Mr Goon on the helmet. He turned a beetroot colour, and the boys fled.

'Toads!' muttered Mr Goon, mopping his hot neck. 'Toads! Anyone would think this was their case! Anyone would think they were running the whole show. Under my feet the whole time. Gah!'

He strode up the path to the front door. But the old lady had now gone to sleep, and did not waken even when Mr Goon spoke to her loudly. He saw the oilskin on the peg, and the same thought occurred to him, as had occurred to the two boys. Big oilskin – Big man – Big feet – The thief!

He crept in and began to look round. He fell over a shovel and the old woman awoke in a hurry. She saw Mr Goon and screamed.

'Help! Help! Robbers! Thieves! Help, I say!'

Mr Goon was scared. He stood up, and spoke pompously. 'Now, madam, it's only the police come to call. What size shoes does your son take?'

This was too much for the old woman. She thought the policeman must be crazy. She began to rock herself so violently that Mr Goon was sure the chair would fall over.

He took one last look round and ran, followed by the old woman's yells. He leapt on his bicycle and was off up the lane in a twinkling. Poor Mr Goon – he was no match for an angry old woman!

15. MOSTLY ABOUT BOOTS

Fatty had gone off to find Colonel Cross's house. It was a pleasant little place not far from the river. Sitting out in the garden was a big man with a white moustache and a very red face.

Fatty studied him from the shelter of the hedge. He looked a bit fierce. In fact, very fierce. It was quite a good thing he was asleep, Fatty thought. Not only asleep, but snoring.

Fatty looked at his feet. Enormous! The cobbler was right – the Colonel certainly wore size twelve or thirteen boots. Fatty thought he could see a rubber heel on one of them too. Goodness – suppose he had at last hit on the right person! But Colonel Cross didn't look in the least like a thief or burglar. Anything but, thought Fatty.

Fatty wished he had a small telescope or long-sighted glasses so that he could look more closely at the rubber heel. He didn't dare to go crawling into the garden and look at the heels. The Colonel was certainly very fast asleep, one leg crossed over the other – but he might be one of those light sleepers that woke very suddenly!

The Colonel did wake suddenly. He gave an extra loud snore and woke himself up with a jump. He sat up, and wiped his face with a tablecloth of a handkerchief. He certainly was enormous. He suddenly caught sight of Fatty's face over the hedge and exploded.

'Did you wake me up? What are you doing there? Speak up, man!'

'I didn't wake you, sir,' said Fatty, in a humble voice. 'I was just looking at your feet.'

'Bless us all – my feet? What for?' demanded the Colonel.

'I was wishing you had an old pair of your boots to give me,' said Fatty, very humbly. 'I'm an old tramp, sir, and tramping's hard on the feet. Very hard, sir. And I've big feet, sir, and it's hard to get boots to fit me – cast-off boots, I mean.'

'Go round and ask my housekeeper,' said the Colonel gruffly. 'But see you do something in return if there's an old pair to give you! Hrrrrrumph!'

This was a wonderful noise – rather like what a horse makes. Fatty stored it away for future use. Hrrrrrump! Fine! He would startle the others with it one day.

'Thank you, sir. I'll chop up wood or do anything if I can have a pair of your boots!' he said.

He left the hedge and went round to the back door. A kindly-faced woman opened it.

'Good day, Ma'am, the Colonel says have you got a pair of his old boots for me?' asked Fatty, his hat in his hands, so that his straggly grey hair showed.

'Another old soldier!' sighed the housekeeper. 'There's not a pair of boots – but there may be an old pair of shoes. And even so, they're not really worn out yet! Dear me – the Colonel only came back yesterday and here he is giving his things away as usual!'

Fatty pricked up his ears. 'Where has he been?' he asked.

'Oh, India,' said the woman. 'And now he's home for the last time. Arrived by air yesterday.'

Ah, thought Fatty, then that rules out the Colonel. Not that I really thought it could be him

– he doesn't look in the least like a burglar! Still, all suspects have to be examined, all clues have to be followed.

The woman came back with a pair of old shoes. They had rubber heels on. Fatty's eyes gleamed when he saw them. The pattern of the heels looked extremely like the pattern he had drawn in his notebook! How interesting!

'Did you say you often give your master's shoes away?' he asked.

'Not only shoes – anything,' she said. 'He's fierce, you know, but he's kind too – always handing out things to his old soldiers. But since he's been away, I've sent his things to the jumble sales each year.'

'My – I hope you didn't send any of this size boots or shoes!' said Fatty jokingly. 'They would have done fine for me!'

'I sent a pair of boots last year,' said the woman, 'they would just have done for you. But who would buy such enormous ones, I *don't* know. I said to Miss Kay when she asked me for them, "Well there now, you can have them, but you won't sell them, I'll wager!" '

Fatty made a mental note to find Miss Kay and ask her if she remembered who bought the big boots belonging to the Colonel. It might have been the thief!

'The Colonel said I was to do a job for you,' said Fatty remembering.

'Well now, you go and weed that bed out in the garden,' said the housekeeper. 'I can't seem to get down to it. He's asleep again. I can hear him snoring, so you won't disturb him.'

'I'll be pleased to do it,' said the old tramp and shuffled off. The housekeeper stared after him. He seemed so feeble that she felt rather guilty at having asked him to weed that bed!

Fatty knelt down and began to weed. He spent a pleasant ten minutes pulling out groundsel and chickweed, and in sorting out the thoughts in his head. He was beginning to think that the clues of '2 Frinton' and '1 Rods' were not clues at all – simply bits of paper blown by chance into the Norton House garden. The real clues were the big footprints and gloveprints – and perhaps the strange print with the criss-cross marks on it.

Still, if the Colonel's boots led him to the thief

who had bought them, the scraps of paper would have come in useful after all, Fatty thought swiftly as he weeded.

He heard the sound of bicycle tyres on the lane outside. The sound stopped as someone got off the bicycle. A head looked cautiously over the hedge. Fatty looked up at the same moment.

Goon was peering over the hedge! He saw Fatty at the same moment as Fatty saw him, and gave a startled grunt. That tramp! He'd left him asleep on the bench outside his house – and now here he was weeding in the Colonel's garden. Goon couldn't believe his eyes.

Fatty nodded and smiled amiably. Goon's eyes nearly dropped out of his head. He felt very angry. Everywhere he went there was somebody before him – first those girls, then those boys, now this deaf, old, dirty tramp. If Goon had been a dog he would have growled viciously.

'What are *you* doing here?' said Goon, in a low, hoarse voice.

'Weeding,' answered Fatty, forgetting to be deaf. 'Nice job, weeding.'

'Any cheek from you,' began Goon, forgetting

not to wake the Colonel. But it was too late. Colonel Cross awoke once more with a jump. He sat up and mopped his forehead. Then he caught sight of Goon's brilliant red face over the top of the hedge. Goon was still addressing Fatty.

'What you doing in this neighbourhood?' Goon was saying aggressively.

The Colonel exploded. 'What's that! What's that! Are you addressing me, my man? What are *you* doing, I should like to know! Hrrrrrumph!'

The last noise startled Goon very much. Fatty chortled as he weeded.

'It's all right, sir. I was speaking to that tramp,' said Goon, with dignity. 'I – er – I had occasion to speak sternly to him this morning, sir. Can't have loiterers and tramps around – what with robberies and things.'

'I don't know what you're talking about,' said Colonel Cross. 'Go away. Policemen should know better than to come and wake me up by shouting to tramps who have been given a job in my garden.'

'I came to have a word with you, actually, sir,' said Goon, desperately. 'Privately.'

147

'If you think I'm going to get up and go indoors and hear a lot of nonsense from you about robberies and tramps and loiterers, you're wrong,' said the old Colonel fiercely. 'If you've got something to say, say it here! That old tramp won't understand a word.'

Fatty chortled to himself again. Goon cleared his throat. 'Well – er – I – came, sir – just to ask you about your boots!'

'Mad,' said the Colonel, staring at Goon. 'Mad! Must be the hot weather! Wants to talk about my boots! Go away and lie down. You're mad!'

Goon was afraid to go on with the matter. He wheeled his bicycle down the lane, and waited a little while to see if the old tramp came out. He meant to have a word with him! Ho! He'd teach him to cheek him in the Colonel's garden!

Fatty finished the bed and tiptoed out, because the Colonel was once more asleep. He said good day to the housekeeper, and went off down the path with the old pair of shoes slung round his neck. He was longing for a moment to open his notebook and compare the pattern of those rubber heels!

He didn't see Mr Goon till he was almost on top

of him. Then the policeman advanced on him, with fire in his eye. He stopped short when he saw the enormous pair of shoes slung round Fatty's neck.

To think he'd come all the way down there to talk politely to the Colonel about his boots, and had been ordered off and told he was mad – and this dirty old tramp had actually begged a pair, and was wearing them round his neck! Shoes that might be great big clues!

'Give me those!' ordered Goon, and grabbed at the shoes. But the feeble, shuffling old tramp twisted cleverly out of the way, and raced off down the road as if he was a schoolboy running in a race.

As indeed he was! Fatty put on his fastest speed, and raced away before Mr Goon had recovered sufficiently from his surprise even to mount his bicycle.

Fatty turned a corner and hurled himself through a hedge into a field. He tore across it, knowing that Goon couldn't ride his bicycle there. He would have to go a long way round to cut him off!

Across the field, over the stile, across another

field, down a lane, round a corner – and here was the front gate of his own house! Into the gate and down the path to the shed. The cook caught a brief glimpse of a tramp-like figure from the kitchen window and then it was gone. She hardly knew if she had seen it or not.

Fatty sank down in the shed, panting, and then got up again to lock the door. Phew! What a run! Goon was well and truly left behind. Now to examine the rubber heels.

16. ON THE TRACK AT LAST!

Fatty pulled out his notebook and turned over its pages eagerly till he came to the drawings he had made of the footprints. He glued his eyes to his sketch of the pattern of the rubber heel shown in one of the prints.

'Line going across there, two little lines under it, long one there, and three lines together,' he noted. Then he compared the drawn pattern with the rubber heel on one of the shoes.

'It's the same!' he said exultingly. 'The absolute same! That proves it – although it's not the Colonel, it's somebody who wears his old boots – somebody who bought a pair last year at Miss Kay's jumble sale. I'm on the track at last!'

He was thrilled. After all their goings and comings, their watchings and interviewings, which seemed to have come to nothing, at *last* they had something to work on. Something Mr Goon hadn't got!

Fatty did a solemn little jig round his shed. He looked very comical indeed, for he was still disguised as a tramp. He carried one of the big shoes in each hand and waved them about gracefully, as if he was doing a scarf or flower dance.

He heard a sound at the window, and stopped suddenly. Was it Mr Goon? Or his mother?

It was neither. It was Larry's grinning face, enjoying the spectacle of the old tramp's idiotic dance. Fatty rushed to the door and unlocked it. All the others were there, smiling to see Fatty's excitement.

'What is it, Fatty? You've got good news,' said Daisy, pleased.

'I must get these things off,' said Fatty, pulling off his grey wig and suddenly appearing forty years younger. 'Phew – a wig's very hot in this weather! Now, report to me, all of you, while I make myself decent.'

They all made their reports. First the girls, who giggled when they told him of the boots and shoes they had got from the Rodneys for the jumble sale. 'We've taken them already to give to Miss

Kay, the person who's running it,' said Daisy. 'Oh dear – if you could have seen Mr Goon's face when he saw us staggering out with loads of shoes and boots! Anyway, there's nobody at the Rodneys with big feet, so that's another clue finished with. I don't somehow think those scraps of paper meant anything.'

'Nor do I,' said Larry. 'We got mixed up with old Clear-Orf too – he arrived at Rodways when we were there. He nearly had a heart attack when he saw us, he was so furious! We really thought we'd got something at that place though, when we saw a colossal sou'wester and oilskin hanging up. But no – the owner wears small-size shoes after all!'

'Now tell us what you did down at Colonel Cross's,' said Daisy expectantly. 'Go on, Fatty!'

Fatty related his tale with gusto, and when he came to the bit where he had looked up from his weeding and seen Mr Goon's face glowering over the hedge, with the sleeping Colonel between them, the others went off into fits of helpless laughter.

'Oh, Fatty – if only I'd been there!' said Daisy. 'What about the shoes? Tell us.'

Fatty told them everything, and proudly

displayed the shoes. 'And now the greatest news of all!' he said, turning up the shoes suddenly so that they displayed the rubber heels. 'See the rubbers? Well, look!'

He placed his notebook down beside one of the shoes, so that the drawing and the rubber heel were side-by-side. The children exclaimed at once.

'It's the same pattern! The very same! Golly, we're getting somewhere now. But surely – it can't be the Colonel who's got anything to do with the robbery?'

'No,' said Fatty, and explained about how a pair of his boots had been sent to last year's jumble sale. 'And *if* we can find out who bought them, I think we've got our hands on the thief!' said Fatty exultingly. 'We shall find that the person who bought them is somebody else with big feet – somebody the cobbler doesn't know about because probably the fellow mends his own boots. We're on the track at last!'

Everyone felt thrilled. They watched Fatty become his own self again, rubbing away the greasy lines on his face, removing his eyebrows carefully, sliding his aching feet out of the stiff old boots he wore. He grunted and groaned as he took off the boots and rubbed his sore feet.

'I had three pairs of socks on,' he said, 'because the boots are so big and stiff – but even so, I bet I'll limp for days!'

'You do everything so thoroughly, Fatty,' said Bets admiringly, watching him become the Fatty she knew.

'Secret of success, Bets,' said Fatty with a grin. 'Now then – what do we do next? I feel that our next move is very, very important – and it's got to be done quickly before old Mr Goon gets another move on.'

Daisy gave a little giggle when she remembered how they had seen through Mr Goon's disguise that morning, and pestered him. Poor old Clear-Orf! 'Please can you tell us the time?', 'Please can you give us change?' Oh dear – however dared they be such pests!

'Anyone know Miss Kay?' asked Fatty, putting on his shoes and lacing them up. 'She apparently ran the jumble sale last year. Is she running it this year?'

'Yes,' said Daisy. 'She's the one we took the Rodneys' shoes to. But, Fatty, we can't very well go barging up to her and ask her straight out who bought those boots of the Colonel's last year – she'd think it awfully strange.'

'I'm not thinking of doing any barging or blurting out of silly questions,' said Fatty with dignity. 'I've got a very fine idea already – no barging about it!'

'Of *course* Fatty's got a good idea,' said Bets, loyally. 'He always has. What is it, Fatty?'

'I'm simply going to present our very finest clue to Miss Kay for her jumble sale – the Colonel's big shoes – and mention casually that perhaps the person who bought them last year, whoever he was, might like to buy the same size again this year!' said Fatty. 'Same kind of rubber heels and all!'

Everyone gazed admiringly at him. That was about the best and most direct way of getting the vital information they wanted, without arousing any suspicion at all! Trust Fatty to produce an idea like that.

'Very good, Fatty,' said Pip, and the others agreed.

'Let's have tea now,' said Fatty, looking at the time. 'I'll go and see if I can get something out of our cook. You come with me, Bets, because she likes you – and we'll take it out under that tree over there and have a picnic, and relax a bit after all our hard work today.'

He and Bets went off together. They came back with an enormous tea on two trays, and an excited Buster. The cook had looked after him all day, and kept him from following Fatty; now he was wild with delight to be with his friends again.

'It's a marvel both the trays haven't crashed,' said Fatty, putting his down carefully. 'I never knew such a dog for getting under your feet when you're carrying anything heavy. Get away from that cake, Buster. Daisy, do stop him licking it all over. There'll be no icing left. Oh golly, now he's stepped on the buns.'

Bets caught Buster and held him down beside her. 'He can't help dancing about, he's so pleased we're back,' she said. 'See what lovely things we've brought you all! I feel we've earned a good tea!'

They talked over their day as they ate, giggling whenever they thought of poor Mr Goon and his despair at finding them just in front of him, wherever he went.

'I'm going down to Miss Kay's this evening,' said Fatty. 'Taking the shoes! Oh, wonderful, magnificent shoes that will solve the mystery for us! And before seven o'clock comes, I'll be back with the name of the thief! A little telephoning to the Inspector – and a little explaining – and we shall be able to let Mr Goon know tomorrow that the case is closed – the mystery is solved – as usual, by the Five Find-Outers – and Dog!'

'Hip, hip, hurrah!' said Pip. 'I say, Bets – *don't* give Buster any more of those potted-meat sandwiches – I want some too! Fatty, stop her. Buster's fat enough as it is. If he gets much fatter he won't be able to help in any more mysteries. Not that he's *really* helped in this one much!'

'Now you've made him put his tail down,' said Bets, and gave him another sandwich. 'Oh, Fatty, do let me come with you to Miss Kay's. You know who she is, don't you? She's the cousin of that horrid little baker – the one who always tries to be funny.'

'She's just as silly as he is,' said Daisy. 'I told you that we took the Rodneys' boots and shoes to her this afternoon. She's got a dreadful collection of things there. Honestly, I think jumble is awful. She was very pleased with the boots and shoes. She says they go like hot cakes at a sale.'

'Well, I think I'll go now,' said Fatty, getting up and brushing the crumbs from his front. 'Coming, Bets? Yes, you can come too, Buster.'

Bets, Buster and Fatty went out. Fatty carried the Colonel's shoes wrapped in a bit of brown paper.

'Well, so long!' said Fatty cheerfully. 'Get out the flags for when we come back – we'll bring you the name of the thief!'

17. A BITTER DISAPPOINTMENT

Fatty and Bets walked off to Miss Kay's with Buster trotting at their heels. They kept a sharp lookout for Mr Goon. Fatty felt sure that he had guessed who the old tramp was that afternoon, and he didn't particularly want to meet him just then.

Miss Kay lived in a tiny cottage next to her cousin and his wife. Bets hoped they wouldn't see the little baker. 'I get so tired of trying to smile at his silly jokes,' she said to Fatty. 'Look – here we are – don't you think it looks like a place where jumble is taken? Daisy and I thought so, anyway.'

Bets was right. The cottage and its little garden looked untidy and 'jumbly', as Bets put it. A broken-down seat was in the little front garden, and a little, much-chipped statue stood in the centre. The gate was half off its hinges, and one of its bars had gone. The curtains at the window looked dirty and didn't match.

'I should think Miss Kay buys most of the jumble for herself!' whispered Bets, nodding at the broken seat and chipped statue.

Miss Kay looked a bit of a jumble herself when she opened the door to them. She was as small and sprightly as her baker-cousin, but not nearly so neat and spruce. 'She's all bits and pieces,' thought Bets, looking at her. 'Hung about with all the jumble nobody else buys – bead necklaces, a torn scarf, a belt with its embroidery spoilt, and that awful red comb in her hair!'

Miss Kay seemed delighted to see them. '*Do* come in!' she said, in a kind of cooing voice. 'It isn't often I get a nice young gentleman to see me. And this dear little girl again too – you came this afternoon, didn't you, dearie?'

'Yes,' said Bets, who didn't like being called 'dearie' by Miss Kay.

'And what have you brought me *this* time, love?' asked Miss Kay, leading the way into a little room so crowded with furniture that Fatty had great difficulty in finding where to step. He knocked over a small table, and looked down in alarm.

'I'm so sorry,' he said, and bent to pick up the things that had fallen. Miss Kay bent down at the same time and their heads bumped together.

'Oh, sorry,' said Fatty again. Miss Kay gave a little giggle, and rubbed her head.

'Oh, it's nothing! My cousin says I've got a wooden head, so a bump never matters to me!' She gave another silly little giggle, and Bets smiled feebly.

'This kind little girl brought me *such* a lot of nice things for the jumble sale this afternoon,' chattered Miss Kay. 'And I'm hoping *you've* brought something too. *What's* in that parcel?'

She put her head on one side, and her comb fell out. She gave a little squeal and picked it up. 'Oh dear – I seem to be falling to bits! You know, that cheeky cousin of mine says one day I'll be a bit of jumble myself, and be sold for a penny. He, he, he!'

Fatty felt rather sick. He didn't like the baker, her cousin, but he liked Miss Kay even less. He opened his parcel and took out the shoes. All he wanted to do now was to get the information he needed, and go!

Miss Kay gave another squeal. 'Oh! *What* an

enormous pair of shoes! Are they *yours*? That's just a joke of course, I didn't mean it. I'm such a tease, aren't I? My, it's quite a good pair though.'

'It's a pair of Colonel Cross's,' said Fatty. 'He sent a pair of boots last year too. I thought perhaps the same person who had feet big enough to fit last year's boots would probably like to buy these. Do you know who it was?'

Bets' heart began to beat fast. She looked breathlessly at Miss Kay. She and Fatty waited for the name. What would it be?

'Oh, they weren't sold last year,' said Miss Kay. 'There was *quite* a little mystery about them! Really it gave me *quite* a shock. You see . . .'

'What do you mean – they weren't sold?' asked Fatty, determined to keep her to the point.

'Well, love – they just *disappeared*!' said Miss Kay, speaking with bated breath as if she hardly wanted anyone to hear. 'Disappeared! One night they were here, ready for the sale – and the next morning they were gone!'

'Were they stolen?' asked Fatty, bitterly disappointed.

'Oh yes – no doubt about it,' said Miss Kay. 'Funny thing is, nothing else was taken at all – just

163

those big boots. They were under that table over there – where I've put all the boots and shoes this year – and the thief went there, picked out the big boots and went off with them. I'd marked them with a price and everything. As a matter-of-fact, I hoped to sell them to that nice policeman of ours – Mr Goon. But they just went one night.'

'Who stole them – do you know?' asked Fatty. 'Is there anyone you know who has big feet, who might think of stealing them? It must surely be someone in the village – how else would they know you had a pair of enormous boots here that would fit them? They knew where to find them too – under that table in your cottage!'

Miss Kay gave another little squeal. 'How very clever you are, love! As clever as that nice Mr Goon. No, I don't know who took the boots – and I don't know anyone with enormous feet either, who could wear them.'

'Did Mr Goon know about it?' asked Fatty.

'Oh no. My cousin said that as I'd only marked the boots cheaply, it wasn't worth taking up the time of the police over a pair of jumble boots,' said Miss Kay. 'He's very good like that, my cousin is.

He gave me some money towards the stolen boots and I gave some myself, and we put the money into the jumble box, so the sale didn't lose by it. I do hope you think I was right.'

'Quite right,' said Fatty, bored with all this niggling over jumble boots, and wild to think that their wonderful idea was no good. The boots had been stolen – and nobody knew who had taken them. Nobody even seemed to know anyone with outsize feet. There seemed to be a dearth of large feet in Peterswood. It was really most annoying. He seemed to run into a blank wall, no matter what clue he followed. Fatty felt very down in the dumps.

'I think, on the whole, I won't leave these big shoes here,' said Fatty, wrapping them up again. 'I mean – if there are thieves about here who have an urge for enormous boots and shoes, these might disappear as well. I'll bring them down to you on the day of the jumble sale, Miss Kay.'

Fatty wasn't going to leave his precious shoes, with their rubber heels, at Miss Kay's now that he hadn't got the information he wanted! It would be a waste of his clue. He was quite determined about that.

Miss Kay looked as if she was going to burst into tears. Fatty hurriedly went to the door with Bets before this disaster happened. He saw someone in the next garden – the little baker, Miss Kay's cousin. He groaned. Now there would be another volley of silly talk.

'Hello, hello, *hello*!' said the baker genially. 'If it isn't Frederick Trotteville, the great detective. Solved the mystery of the robbery yet, young man?'

Fatty always hated being called 'young man' and he especially disliked it from the little baker. He scowled.

Bets spoke up for him. 'He's nearly solved it. He soon will. We just want to find the name of the man with big feet, that's all. We almost got it tonight.'

'Shut up, Bets,' said Fatty in a low and most unexpectedly cross voice. Bets flushed and fell silent. But the little baker made up for her sudden silence.

'Well, well, well – we shall expect to hear great things soon! I suppose the same man did both the robberies? I saw his prints all right! Me and Mr Goon, we had a good old chinwag over it – ah, Mr Goon will get the thief all right – before you do, young man! He's on the track, yes, he's on the track. Told me so when I left his bread today. Those were his very words. "I'm on the track, Twit," he said, just like that.'

'Interesting,' said Fatty in a bored voice, and opened the gate for Bets to go through. The little baker didn't like Fatty's tone of voice. He strutted up to his own gate and stood there, going up and down on his heels in rather an insolent manner, leering at Bets and Fatty.

' "Interesting!" you says – just like that! Pride goes before a fall, young man. You watch your step. I've heard a lot about you from Mr Goon.'

'That's enough, Twit,' said Fatty in such a stern, grown-up voice that Bets jumped. So did Twit. He altered his tone at once.

'I didn't mean no harm. Just my joke, like. Me and my cousin, Miss Kay, we do like a joke, don't we, Coz?'

Coz was apparently Miss Kay, who was standing by her front gate, smiling and listening, bobbing up and down on her heels just like her cousin.

'Guard your tongue, Twit,' said Fatty, still in his grown-up voice. 'You'll get yourself into trouble if you don't.'

He walked off with Bets, angry, disappointed, and rather crestfallen. Twit and Miss Kay watched them go. Twit was red in the face and angry.

'Insolence!' he said to his cousin. 'Young upstart! Talking to me like that! I'll learn him. Thinks himself very clever, does he? Ah, Mr Goon's right – he's a toad, that boy.'

'Oh, don't talk like that!' said Miss Kay fearfully. 'You'll lose your customers!'

Bets slipped her hand through Fatty's arm as they went home. 'Fatty,' she said, 'I'm awfully sorry for what I said to Twit. I didn't think it mattered.'

'Well, I suppose it doesn't,' said Fatty, patting Bets' hand. 'But never talk when we're solving a mystery, Bets. You just might give something away – though it seems to me that Twit must know pretty well everything from Mr Goon – they sound like bosom friends!'

'Are you very disappointed, Fatty?' asked Bets, very sad to see Fatty so down in the dumps. It wasn't like him.

'Yes, I am,' said Fatty. 'We've come to a dead end, little Bets. There's no further clue to follow, nothing more to do. We'll have to give it up – the first mystery we've ever been beaten by!'

And, in a mournful silence, the two went dolefully down to the shed to tell the miserable news.

18. THE THIRD ROBBERY

For a day or two, the Five Find-Outers were very much subdued. It was horrid to have to give up – just when they had thought the whole thing was going to be solved so quickly and successfully too!

Fatty was quite upset by it. He worried a lot, going over and over all the clues and the details of the two robberies, trying to find another trail to follow. But he couldn't. As he had said to Bets, they had come to a dead end, a blank wall.

The weather broke and the rain came down. What with that and Fatty looking so solemn, the other four were quite at a loose end. They got into mischief, irritated their parents, and simply didn't know what to do with themselves.

Fatty cheered up after a bit. 'It's just that I *hate* being beaten, you know,' he said to the others. 'I never am, as a matter-of-fact. This is the first time

– and if anybody feels inclined to say, "Well, I suppose it's good for you, Fatty," I warn them, don't say it. It *isn't* good for me. It's bad.'

'Well, do cheer up now, Fatty,' said Daisy. 'It's really awful having you go about looking like a hen out in the rain! As for poor old Buster, I hardly know if he's got a tail these days, it's tucked between his legs so tightly. It hasn't wagged for days!'

'Hey, Buster! Good dog, Buster! I'm all right now!' said Fatty suddenly, to the little Scottie. He spoke in his old cheerful voice, and Buster leapt up as if he had been shot. His tail wagged nineteen to the dozen, he barked, flung himself on Fatty and then went completely mad.

He tore round and round Pip's playroom as if he was running a race, and finally hurled himself out of the door, slid all the way down the landing, and fell down the stairs.

The children screamed with delight. Buster was always funny when he went mad. Mrs Hilton's voice came up the stairs.

'Pip! Fatty! Come and catch Buster. He seems to have gone off his head. Oh – here he comes again. What *is* the matter with him?'

Buster tore up the stairs at sixty miles an hour, slid along the landing again and came to rest under a chair. He lay there, panting, quite tired out, his tail thumping against the floor.

Everyone felt better after that. Fatty looked at his watch. 'Let's go to Oliver's again and have a splash – I could do with three or four meringues.'

'Ooooh, yes – *I've* got some money today,' said Larry, pulling out some money. 'My Uncle Ted gave me it weeks ago and I couldn't think where I'd put it for safety. I found it today in my tie-box.'

'We'll all go shares,' said Pip. 'I've got two pounds, and Bets has got one.'

'Right,' said Fatty. 'The more the merrier. Come on. I'll just telephone my mother to tell her we're going to Oliver's.'

They went off, feeling happier than they had done for days. Buster's tail had appeared again and was wagging merrily as he ran along with them. His master was all right again – life was bright once more!

They stayed a long time over their tea, talking hard, and eating equally hard. Nobody said a word about the mystery. They weren't going to remember defeat when éclairs and meringues and chocolate cake were spread in front of them! That would be silly.

Feeling rather full, they walked back to Fatty's and went down the garden to the shed. Buster trotted on ahead. He surprised them all by suddenly barking urgently and loudly.

'What's up, Buster?' shouted Fatty, beginning to run. Larry raced down the path with him. Whatever could Buster be barking about like that?

Pip and Larry came to the shed. The door was wide open, though Fatty always left it shut and locked. Fatty ran in, amazed. He looked round.

His things were all in a muddle! Clothes had been dragged down from the pegs, drawers in a chest had been emptied, and everywhere was mess and muddle. Someone had been there and turned everything upside down.

'My money's gone, of course,' said Fatty in exasperation. 'I'd got two pounds I was saving for Mummy's birthday – why did I leave it here! I never do leave money in the ordinary way. Blow!'

'Anything else gone?' asked Larry. Pip, Daisy

and Bets crowded into the untidy shed. Bets burst into tears, but nobody took any notice of her, not even Fatty.

'My knife's gone – that silver one,' said Fatty. 'And that little silver case I kept odds and ends in. And yes – my cigarette case is gone, the one I use when I'm disguised. Well, the thief is welcome to that! I suppose he thought it was silver, but it isn't!'

'Oh, Fatty!' wailed Bets. 'What's happened? Has a robber been here? Oh, what shall we do?'

She went outside to swallow her tears and be sensible – and then she suddenly saw something that made her stare. She yelled loudly.

'Fatty! FATTY! Come here, quick!'

Fatty appeared at top speed, the others behind him. Bets pointed to the muddy path near the shed. On it were clear footprints – enormous ones!

'Gosh!' said Fatty. 'It's our robber again. The very same one – look at the marks his rubber heels made – the same pattern as before.'

'Will there be gloveprints too?' asked Daisy excitedly, and she went back into the shed.

'Shouldn't think so,' said Fatty following. 'There's no wallpaper or paint to show them up.'

'Well, look – there they are!' said Daisy, pointing triumphantly. And sure enough, there were two large gloveprints showing clearly on the looking-glass that Fatty had in his shed!

'He likes to leave his mark, doesn't he?' said Larry. 'You'd almost think he was saying, "This is the robber, his mark!"'

'Yes,' said Fatty thoughtfully. 'Well, it's the same fellow all right. He hasn't got away with a great deal, thank goodness – but what a mess!'

'We'll soon clear it up,' said Bets, eager to do something for poor old Fatty.

'Let's take a very, very careful snoop round before we move *any*thing,' said Fatty. 'The mystery has come right to our very door – it's all-alive-oh again. We may perhaps be able to solve it this time.'

'I suppose you're not going to inform the police!' said Larry with a laugh.

'No. I'm not,' said Fatty very firmly. 'First thing I'm going to do is to measure the footprints to make absolutely certain they're the same ones that we saw before – at Norton House and at Mrs Williams's.'

They were, of course, exactly the same. No

doubt about it at all. The gloveprints were the same too.

'We can't find out whether there was a hollow cough this time,' said Pip, 'because there was nobody here to hear it. I suppose there aren't any scraps of paper, are there, Fatty?'

'None,' said Fatty. 'But there weren't at Mrs Williams's either, you know. I'm beginning to think that they really had nothing to do with the robberies. They don't really link up with anything.'

Daisy went wandering off down the path a little. She came to another print by the side of the path, almost under a shrub. She called Fatty.

'Look!' she said. 'Isn't this strange print like the ones you found in both the other robberies?'

Fatty knelt to see. On the wet ground under the shrub the mark was quite plain – a big roundish print with criss-cross lines here and there.

'Yes,' said Fatty puzzled, turning over the pages of his notebook to compare his drawing with the print. 'It's the same. I cannot *imagine* what makes it – or why it appears in all the robberies. It's extraordinary.'

They all gazed down at the strange mark. Pip

wrinkled his forehead. 'You know – somehow I feel as if I've seen it somewhere else besides the robberies. Where could it have been?'

'Think, Pip,' said Fatty. 'It might help.'

But Pip couldn't think. All he could say was that he thought he had seen it somewhere on the day when they all went interviewing.

'That's not much help,' said Fatty with a sigh. 'We were all over the place that day. Now we'd better put everything back. I can't see that we can find any more clues. As a matter-of-fact, it seems as if this robbery is almost an exact repetition of the others – large footprints, gloveprints, strange unknown print, and small goods stolen.'

They hung up the clothes, and put back everything into the chest of drawers. They kept a sharp lookout for any possible clue, but as far as they could see there was none at all.

'How did the thief get down to the shed?' asked Larry. 'Did he get in through the back gate leading into the lane, do you think? It's not far from the shed. Or did he come down the path from the house?'

'Well – if he made that mark under the shrub,

it rather looks as if he came from the house,' said Fatty. 'On the other hand, the large footprints are only round and about the shed – I didn't find any on the path up to the house, did you?'

'No,' said Larry. 'Well, it's more likely he would have come quietly in through the back gate down by the shed – he wouldn't be seen then. It's very secluded down here at the bottom of the garden – can't be seen from the house at all.'

'All the same, I think we'd better ask the cook and the maid if they saw anyone,' said Fatty. 'They just might have. And we'll ask who has been to the house this afternoon too. Any tradesman or visitor who might have seen somebody.'

'Yes. Good idea,' said Larry. 'Come on – let's go and find out.'

19. THE WARNING

The maid was out, and had been out all afternoon. The cook was in, however, and was rather surprised to see all five children and Buster trooping in at her kitchen door.

'Now don't you say you want tea,' she began. 'It's a quarter to six, and . . .'

'No, we don't want tea,' said Fatty. 'I just came to ask you a few things. Someone's been disturbing my belongings in the shed at the bottom of the garden. I wondered if you had seen anyone going down the path to the shed this afternoon.'

'Goodness,' said the cook, alarmed. 'Don't tell me there's tramps about again. I thought I saw a very nasty-looking fellow slipping down that path the other day.'

Fatty knew who *that* was all right. So did the others. They turned away to hide their grins.

'No – it's today I want to know about,' said Fatty. 'Did you see anyone at all?'

'Not a soul today,' said the cook. 'And I've been sitting here at this window all the time!'

'You didn't have forty winks, I suppose?' asked Fatty, with a smile. 'You do sometimes.'

'Well, maybe I did for a few minutes,' said the cook with a laugh. 'I get really sleepy in the afternoons, when it's hot like this. Still, I was awake all right when the tradespeople came.'

'Who came?' asked Larry.

'Oh, the usual ones,' said the cook. 'The girl with the groceries, the milkman, the baker – and let me see, did the gasman come? No, that was this morning.'

'Anyone else?' asked Fatty.

'Well, Mr Goon called,' said the cook, 'and he asked for your mother, but she wasn't in. So he went away again. He came at the same time as the baker did. They had a good old talk together too, out in the front garden. I heard them. Mr Goon bumped into the baker just as he was leaving.'

'I bet they had a good talk about Bets and me,' said Fatty to the others. 'Anyone else call, Cook?'

'Not that I know of,' she said. 'I didn't have any talk with the baker – he's too much of a saucy one for me – I just left a note on the table to tell him how many loaves to leave. And I didn't see the milkman either – he knows how much to leave. I saw the grocer's girl and she was in a hurry as usual.'

'I wonder what Mr Goon wanted,' said Fatty as they left the kitchen to walk down to the shed again. 'I bet he wants to know if I was the old tramp the other day. As if Mummy would know!'

They were just walking out of the door when Daisy stopped suddenly and looked down at the ground.

'Look!' she said, and pointed.

They all looked – and there, just by the kitchen door, in a wet patch of ground, was the same roundish mark that they had seen under the shrub! The same as they had seen at the two other robberies as well.

'Gosh!' said Fatty staring down. 'The thief did actually come to the kitchen door then! He must have made that mark – but why?'

'Your cook said nobody else came except the

people she mentioned,' said Larry. 'It seems to me as if the thief came here, peeped in and saw the cook asleep, and went down to the shed to do his dirty work.'

'Then why didn't he leave large footprints here?' said Daisy. 'There's only small ones going to and from the bottom of the garden. I looked. There's no large ones at all – no larger than size seven, anyway.'

'It beats me!' said Pip.

It beat them all. Now there had been three separate robberies, all obviously done by the same man, who left exactly the same marks each time – and yet he had never once been seen, though he must really be a very big fellow indeed.

'He's invisible – that's how he can do all these things!' said Daisy. 'I mean – surely *some*body would have seen him *one* of the times. But all he does is come and go, and leave behind foot and gloveprints, and do just what he likes! He must be laughing up his sleeve at all of us.'

'It *can't* be old Mr Goon, can it?' said Bets hopefully. 'He has large feet and hands, and he *has* got a hollow, sheep-like cough, and he really does hate you, Fatty. He came here today too – why couldn't he have slipped down and been spiteful, turning all your things upside down and making a mess?'

'I daresay he'd *like* to,' said Fatty, 'but remember, he was away at the time of the first robbery – and honestly, I don't think he's mad enough to do such idiotic things – I mean, it's sheer dishonesty, robbing people like this, and Mr Goon wouldn't risk his job and his pension. No, rule that right out, Bets.'

'Are you going to ask the milkman and the others if they saw anyone?' asked Bets. Fatty shook his head.

'No. I'm pretty certain now that if the milkman, the baker, or grocer's girl had seen anyone here this afternoon, wandering about in large-size boots they would have told Cook. Anyway, I'm not interviewing that cocky little baker again – wouldn't he be pleased if he knew I'd been robbed! He'd rub his little hands like anything, and rock to and fro on his toes and heels with glee.'

'Yes, he would,' said Bets, rocking to and fro as she remembered how he had gone up and down on his heels. 'Nasty little man. I hope he doesn't hear about this.'

'No one is to,' said Fatty firmly. 'I'm not going to have Mr Goon strolling down the garden and fingering everything in my shed. How he'd love to look through my make-up box, and pick up all my moustaches and eyebrows and wigs!'

'Well, none of us will say a word about this afternoon's do,' said Larry. 'We'll keep the thief guessing! He'll wonder why there's no news of his last robbery.'

'The thief burst the lock on your door, Fatty,' said Bets. 'How will you lock it tonight?'

'I'll slip out and buy a padlock,' said Fatty. 'That will be the easiest thing to do tonight – put a padlock on the door. I'll come with you when you go home. I can get one at the garage – it stays open till seven.'

So, at ten to seven, Fatty and the others strolled up the lane to the garage in the village. They bought a strong little padlock, and came out examining it.

A voice behind them made them jump. It was Mr Goon, starting on his first night-round.

'Ho! A padlock! Maybe you'll need that, Frederick! You'd better be careful.'

Everyone swung round in astonishment. 'What do you mean, Mr Goon?' said Fatty.

'I've had notice that you'll be the next on the robbery list,' said Goon importantly. 'I came to warn your mother this afternoon. Just make sure that everything is well locked up tonight, windows fastened and everything. And have that there pesky little dog of yours in the front hall.'

'What *is* all this about?' said Fatty, hoping that nobody would blurt out anything about the robbery that had already happened that afternoon. 'What nonsense, Mr Goon!'

Mr Goon swelled up a little, and Bets was sure one of his uniform buttons was about to spring off. He fumbled in his breast-pocket and brought out his little notebook. He undid the elastic strap and ran through the pages. Everyone watched in silence.

He took out a scrap of dirty paper, and handed it to Fatty. 'There you are. If that isn't a plain warning I don't know what is. Course, you don't need to take no notice of it at all – and anyway, I'll be sure to be round two or three times tonight to see as everything is all right round at yours.'

Fatty took the scrap of paper. On it, printed in uneven lettering, were three words,

TROTVILLS NEXT. – Bigfeet

Fatty silently passed it round to the others. They knew what Goon didn't know – that the warning was too late. Bigfeet, the robber, had already been to the Trottevilles!

'There you are!' said Mr Goon, enjoying the interest he was causing. 'The impertinence of it! Good as saying "Fat lot of good you are – I'll tell you where I'm going to strike next." Signing himself Bigfeet too. He's got some sauce!'

'Mr Goon, have you got the other scraps of paper on you?' asked Fatty. 'The ones found at Norton House, with "2 Frinton" and "1 Rods" on? It would be useful to compare them.'

Goon gave a scornful little snort. 'Think I didn't compare them, Mr Smarty? 'Course I did. But this here note's in printed capitals and the others aren't. Can't see any likeness at all.'

'I think you're wrong, Mr Goon,' said Fatty, suddenly speaking like a grown-up again. 'And if you like, I'll show you the likeness.'

'Gah,' said Goon in disgust. 'Think you know everything, don't you? Well, I tell you I've compared the three scraps of paper, and this one's different.'

'I don't believe it,' said Fatty.

That stung Mr Goon and he glared. He felt in the little pocket of his notebook and produced the other two notes. He showed them to Fatty, together with the third one. 'See? No likeness at all!' he said triumphantly.

'I'm not thinking of the words written on the papers,' said Fatty. 'I'm thinking of the *paper* they're written *on*. It's exactly the same. Whoever wrote the first notes, wrote this one too. So those first scraps of paper *were* clues after all – though they led to nothing.'

Mr Goon stared at the scraps of paper. Fatty was right. They had obviously been torn from the same notebook or sheets of paper – they were all rather yellowed and the surface was a little fluffy.

Mr Goon cleared his throat. He felt a little awkward. That boy! Always putting him in the wrong. He put the scraps back into his pocketbook.

He cleared his throat again. 'Think I didn't

notice that?' he said. 'Why, it hits you in the eye!'

'It didn't seem to have given you a very hard blow then,' said Fatty. 'Well, I'm not heeding that warning, Mr Goon – so you can sleep in peace tonight! There will be no robbery at the Trottevilles, I can tell you that!'

20. MOSTLY ABOUT GOON

The five children, with Buster, went on their way, Fatty thinking deeply. The others respected his thoughts and said nothing. They came to the corner where they had to part with Larry and Daisy.

'Any orders, Fatty?' said Larry respectfully.

'Er – what? Oh, orders. No, none,' said Fatty, coming out of his trance. 'Sorry to be so goofy all of a sudden. But it's funny, isn't it? – that warning, I mean. Why did the thief send it? He must be really sure of himself – though, of course, he might have sent it to Mr Goon *after* he'd done the job. I just don't understand it.'

'When did Mr Goon get it?' said Daisy. 'I didn't hear him say. Did you ask him?'

'No. I was so surprised to find that the third scrap of paper was the same as the first two, which meant they really did have something to do with the thief, that I didn't ask any of the questions I should,' said Fatty, vexed. 'That means I'll have to go back and get a little more information. Mr Goon will be pleased!'

'Is the mystery on again?' asked Bets.

'Very much on, Bets,' said Fatty. 'Oh very much! Blow Bigfeet! I shall dream about him tonight. It really is a puzzle how that fellow can get about without being noticed – I mean, there's all of us on the watch, and Mr Goon, and the baker, and the grocer's girl, and goodness knows how many other people too, looking for a large-footed man – and yet the fellow has the nerve to walk up the road to my house, go in at one of the front gates, walk up to the kitchen door, and all the way down to the shed, and then out again with his stolen goods – and not a single soul sees him.'

'He *must* be invisible!' said Bets, quite convinced.

'The case of the invisible thief – or the mystery of Bigfeet the robber!' said Fatty. 'It's a funny case this – lots of clues all leading nowhere.'

They said good-bye and parted. Fatty went back to Mr Goon's house. He must find out where that paper had been put when it was delivered, and what time it was sent.

He came to Mr Goon's house. Goon was back again, and was spending an interesting ten minutes trying on a supply of new moustaches that had arrived by post that day.

He was sitting in front of the mirror, twirling a particularly fine moustache when he heard the knock at the front door. He peered out of the window. Ah – that boy. Goon grinned to himself.

He crammed a hat down on his head, frowned, twisted his new moustache up, and leaned out of the window.

'What do you want?' he asked in a deep, rather sinister voice. Fatty looked up and was extremely startled to see the scowling, moustached face above him. In a trice he recognised Goon – there was no mistaking those frog-like eyes. However, if Goon wanted to think he could make himself unrecognisable by adding a moustache and a scowl, Fatty was quite willing to let him.

'Er – good evening,' said Fatty politely. 'Could I speak to Mr Goon? Or is he busy?'

'He's busy,' said the face, in a hollow voice and the moustache twitched up and down.

'Oh, what a pity. It's rather important,' said Fatty.

'I'll see if he'll see you,' said the face, and disappeared. Fatty chuckled. The door opened half a minute later, and Mr Goon appeared, minus scowl and moustache. Actually he felt quite amiable for once. His disguise had deceived that boy – ha, Fatty wasn't as clever as he thought he was!

'Good evening, Mr Goon,' said Fatty. 'Did your friend tell you I wanted to see you?'

'He did,' said Goon. 'What do you want?'

'I forgot to ask you how you got that third note and when,' said Fatty. 'It might be important.'

'I don't know how *or* when it came,' said Mr Goon annoyingly.

'Well – when did you find it?' asked Fatty.

'I was going through some papers in the office,' said Goon, 'and I was lost in them – very important papers they were, see. Well, the milkman and the baker came and left the bread and the milk as usual – and when I came into the kitchen to get myself a cup of tea, I picked up the bottle of milk – and there was the note on top of it!'

'Thank you,' said Fatty. 'So you don't really

know what time it came, except that it must have come after the milkman and baker. Did you hear *them* come?'

As Mr Goon had been fast asleep all afternoon he had heard no one at all, but he wasn't going to tell Fatty that.

'I expect I heard them come,' he said. 'But when I read through official papers – very important ones too – I get lost in them. I daresay the tradesmen came about the usual time – three o'clock or so.'

'Thanks,' said Fatty. 'That's all I wanted to know. You came along to my house then to give us the warning? Our cook told me you came.'

'Yes. I came along at once,' said Goon. 'As was my bounden duty. Pity you won't take no notice of that warning. Still, I'll be along tonight all right.'

'As is your bounden duty!' said Fatty. 'Well, I'll be off. I'm sorry to have disturbed that friend of yours, Mr Goon.'

'Oh, he won't mind,' said Goon, most gratified to find that Fatty apparently hadn't recognised who the 'friend' was.

'Good-looking fellow, isn't he?' said Fatty, innocently. Goon agreed instantly.

'Yes, quite. Fine moustache,' he said.

'Very, very fine,' said Fatty. 'Actually they are what made him good-looking. Without those, he'd have been very plain indeed, in fact, quite ugly. Don't you agree?'

And before poor Mr Goon could find his tongue, Fatty had gone. That boy! Slippery as an eel in all he said and did. Now, exactly what did he mean by those last remarks?

Fatty walked home, deep in thought again. He had his supper by himself because his parents were out, and didn't even notice what a delicious meal the cook had prepared for him, much to her disappointment. He was thinking so very hard.

He went up to his own room after his meal and tried to read a very thrilling mystery story; but his own mystery was much more interesting to him, and after a bit he pushed the book aside and fell into thought again.

What I can't understand is that all the different clues we have *ought* to fit together like a jigsaw puzzle and make a definite picture of the thief, said Fatty to himself. And they don't. They just don't. And yet, if I could find out how to fit them together, I could solve the mystery at once – who the thief is – how he gets about unseen – why he doesn't care whether his prints are all over the place or not – how he gets away with his goods without fear of being detected with them – and, above all, why he sent that warning. That's so boastful, somehow – he must be very, very certain of himself and his powers.

He fell asleep immediately as soon as he got into bed, and then woke up worrying again. Half-asleep and half-awake, he lay there with his mind milling round and round all the clues and details. Things got mixed up in his half-sleeping mind – the milkman's cart and the warning note on the milk bottle – the baker's basket and pairs of large boots – hollow coughs and large moustaches – there was no end to the pictures that came and went in his mind.

Then Buster began to bark! Fatty awoke properly and sat up. Gosh! Did that warning mean the thief was coming to the *house*? thought Fatty, dragging on his dressing-gown. He had imagined that it meant the robbery in the shed. He shot downstairs and opened the front door to let Buster out. The dog had run straight to the door and scraped at it.

'Well, if the thief's outside, you'll give him a shock, Buster,' said Fatty. Buster shot out and disappeared into the front garden. There came an agonised yell.

'Get out! Clear orf! Clear orf, I say!'

Fatty collapsed into laughter. It was poor old Mr Goon out there, solemnly 'doing his bounden duty' in the middle of the night. He had come to see that the Trotteville's house was not already burgled.

'Buster! Come here!' yelled Fatty, and the yell woke his parents, the cook and the maid at once. Everyone crowded on to the landing.

'Frederick! What *is* all this disturbance?' called his father, coming downstairs. Buster was now in Fatty's arms, struggling to go again. Oh, the joy of being let out in the middle of the night and finding Goon's ankles at his mercy! What a wonderful surprise it had been to Buster.

Mr Goon loomed up in the doorway, very angry. 'You set that there dog on me,' he began. 'And me doing my duty, and guarding your property.'

Mrs Trotteville had no time for Mr Goon. 'What does he want?' she called down to Fatty.

'I don't really know,' said Fatty. 'What exactly did you say you wanted, Mr Goon?'

'I don't want anything, as you very well know,' said Mr Goon, in a real temper. 'I was just doing my duty, what with that warning and all . . .'

'What's he talking about?' said Mr Trotteville coming up to the front door.

'About a warning,' said Fatty.

'What warning?' asked Mr Trotteville, quite at sea.

'Why, that warning from Bigfeet,' said Mr Goon in surprise, not realising that Fatty had said nothing to his parents.

'Bigfeet!' said Mr Trotteville. 'Look here, Goon, you come along in the morning and talk about big feet all you like – but not in the middle of the night. You go home to bed.'

Goon snorted, and was about to say something very cutting when Mr Trotteville firmly shut the door. 'Is he mad?' he asked Fatty.

'Not any more than usual,' said Fatty. 'Well, if he comes again, I'll let Buster out – he won't come very often after that!'

But Goon didn't come again. He walked off wrathfully, thinking of all the things he would like to do to that young toad – yes, and to that pest of a dog too.

And me doing my bounden duty, he said to himself. Well, let'em be robbed good and proper – good and proper, is what I say!

21. PIP PLAYS A TRICK

The next morning, Fatty felt very gloomy again. He ate his breakfast in complete silence, much to his mother's surprise.

'Do you feel quite well, Frederick?' she asked him.

'What, Mummy? Oh yes – I'm all right,' said Fatty. 'Just thinking, that's all.'

'I hope you haven't got mixed up in one of those awful mystery affairs again,' said Mrs Trotteville.

Fatty said nothing. He *was* mixed up in one – and he was completely at a loss about it! Three different robberies – one in his own shed – heaps of clues – and no solution at all, unless he made up his mind that the thief was invisible, which was obviously impossible.

The worst of it is, he's laughing up his sleeve at us the whole time, thought Fatty, in exasperation. I feel that it's someone who knows us. Do we know *him*? And he's so jolly certain of himself and his ability to get away unseen that he even has the cheek to warn us where he's going to commit the next robbery.

He thought of his visit to Miss Kay, and his high hopes when he went there. If only those boots hadn't been stolen, everything would have been so easy.

'Frederick, you really must go and get your hair cut this morning,' said Mrs Trotteville. 'It's far too long.'

'All right, Mummy!' said Fatty, who had been expecting this suggestion for the last two weeks. He knew his hair was rather long, but it made disguises a bit easier if his hair was long and he wasn't going to wear a wig. He could pull it about a bit, and make it go different ways under a hat.

'Ring up and make an appointment,' said Mrs Trotteville, 'then you won't have to wait for ages.'

When the others came at ten o'clock to meet in Fatty's shed, and see if anything further had happened, they were met by a gloomy Fatty.

'Got to go and get my hair cut,' he said. 'I'll be back in about half an hour. You can either wait for me here or go and have your first ice cream of the day while I'm at the hairdresser's.'

'All right,' said Larry. 'Anything further happened?'

'Nothing much – except that Mr Goon came in the middle of the night to see if we'd been burgled or not – and I really thought it might be the thief and let old Buster out. Gosh, he was thrilled to find Mr Goon's ankles out there!'

Everyone laughed, and Fatty cheered up a bit. 'Well, what are you going to do? Wait here?' asked Fatty.

'Yes. I think we will,' said Larry. 'We're all a bit short of cash today. We'll laze here under the trees till you come back. Don't be long.'

Fatty went off, still looking gloomy. The others looked at one another. It was not very nice when Fatty was in low spirits. It didn't often happen but when it did, it cast a definite gloom over the party.

'I wish we could do something to cheer Fatty up,' said Bets.

'Well – let's play a trick on him or something,' said Pip.

'Too hot,' said Larry. 'Not enough time either. He'll be back so soon.'

Pip wandered into Fatty's shed. He looked round. He wondered what he could do – dress up and disguise himself so that Fatty wouldn't know him? No, there wasn't time to do that properly.

His eyes fell on the enormous pair of shoes that Fatty had got from Colonel Cross's housekeeper, and had refused to leave with Miss Kay. There they were, hanging on a peg by their laces. Pip looked at them – and an idea came into his head!

He grinned. Gosh, he certainly *had* got an idea – one that would make Fatty and the others sit up properly. He would enjoy himself over this idea. Talk about a little bamboozling!

He took off his rubber shoes and slipped them into his pocket. He took down the big shoes and pulled them on. They slip-slopped about on his feet, but he could just walk in them. Pip went cautiously out of the shed unseen by the others, who were on the other side of a bush.

He knew Fatty would come back through the garden gate not far from the back of the shed. He also knew that there was a bed there that had just been dug over and prepared by the gardener for lettuces.

Pip walked painfully over to the nice smooth bed. He took a few steps this way on the earth, and a few steps that way. Then he stopped to see his footwork – marvellous! It looked for all the world as if Bigfeet the thief had visited them once again, and left his giant-size footprints plainly to be seen!

Pip grinned again. He took a few more steps, treading as hard as he could. Then he walked quietly back to the shed, took off the shoes, and put on his own once more. He'd like to see old Fatty's face when he came back and saw those footprints!

He walked out to the others. 'Shall we go and meet Fatty?' he said. 'Come on. He'd be pleased. It's only a little way.'

'All right,' said Larry, and Bets and Daisy agreed at once.

'I can see Mrs Trotteville in the front garden,' said Pip, peering through the trees. 'We'd better go and say hello to her.'

He didn't want to take the others past his beautifully-prepared footprints. He wanted the full glory of them to burst on everyone at once. He hugged himself gleefully.

They said a few polite words to Mrs Trotteville and then escaped. They walked almost to the hairdresser's before they met Fatty. He came towards them looking very smooth-headed indeed. Buster trotted as usual at his heels.

'Hello – come to meet me?' said Fatty, pleased. 'Right. ice creams for everyone in return!'

'Oh no, Fatty,' said Daisy. 'You're always spending your money on us.'

'Come on,' said Fatty, and they went to have ice creams. Pip sat as patiently as he could with his. He hoped everyone would hurry up. Suppose the gardener went down to that bed and raked over the footprints! His trick would be ruined.

They finished their ice cream at last, and walked back to Fatty's. Pip wished they would hurry, but they wouldn't, of course!

'We'll go in the garden gate way,' said Fatty, as Pip had hoped he would say. 'It's nearer.'

They all went in. The bed with the footprints

was not very far from the gate. Bets was running ahead with Buster when she suddenly saw them. She stopped at once, amazed.

Then Fatty saw them. He stopped dead and stared as if he couldn't believe his eyes. Larry and Daisy looked down in astonishment.

'Gosh!' said Fatty. 'What do you make of *that*! Fresh made too!'

Pip grinned, and tried to hide it – but nobody was looking at him at all. Their eyes were glued to the enormous footprints.

'I *say*! The thief's been here – while we were gone!' said Daisy. 'Just those few minutes!'

'There's the gardener over there – we'll ask him who's been here,' said Fatty. But the gardener shook his head.

'Nobody came down the garden while I've been working here,' he said. 'And I've been here for an hour or more. Never saw a soul!'

'Invisible as usual!' groaned Fatty. 'I just can't make it out. He comes and goes as he likes, does what he likes – and nobody ever sees him.'

He took out a magnifying glass and bent to look closely at the prints. He frowned a little, and then got out his notebook. He opened it at the drawings there. Then he straightened up.

'This is odd,' he said. 'I don't understand it. These prints are the same size – and the rubber heel pattern is the same – but the print isn't *quite* the same. The thief didn't wear the same boots.'

Clever old Fatty! thought Pip. He even spotted that the prints were made by those big shoes, and not by big boots worn by the real thief. He really is a marvel!

The five children walked to the trees and sat down. Pip kept his head turned away because he simply couldn't help grinning all over his face. What a joke! How marvellous to see the others taken in like this – all serious and solemn and earnest!

'It beats me,' said Fatty. 'It absolutely beats me. Running all over the bed like that for apparently no reason at all. He must be mad as well as a thief. I mean – what's the point? Just to show off, I suppose.'

Pip gave a little snort of laughter and tried to turn it into a cough. Bets looked at him in surprise. 'What are you grinning for?' she asked. 'What's the joke?'

'No joke,' said Pip, trying to straighten his face. But a moment later his mouth twisted into broad smiles again and he was afraid he was going to laugh out loud.

'At any moment I shall expect to see footprints suddenly walking in front of me now,' said Fatty gloomily. 'I've really got the things on my mind.'

Pip gave a squeal and burst into laughter. He rolled over on the ground. He laughed till he almost burst his sides. The others looked at him in amazement.

'Pip! What's the joke?' demanded Fatty.

'It's – er – oh dear – I can't tell you,' stuttered Pip, and rolled over again.

'He's gone potty,' said Larry, in disgust. Fatty looked at Pip hard. He poked him with his foot.

'Shut up now, Pip – and tell us what the joke is,' he said. 'Go on – you've been up to something. What is it?'

'Oh my – it's those footprints,' gasped Pip. 'I took you all in beautifully, didn't I!'

'What do you mean?' cried everyone, and Fatty reached out and shook Pip.

'I made them!' said Pip, helpless with laughter. 'I put on those big shoes and made those prints myself!'

22. MEETING AT HALF PAST TWO

Larry, Daisy and Bets fell on Pip until he cried for mercy. Buster joined in and barked madly. Only Fatty did nothing. He just sat as if he was turned to stone.

The others realised at last that Fatty was not joining in Pip's punishment. They sat up and looked at him. Pip wiped his streaked, dirty face.

Fatty sat there as if a thunderbolt had struck him. He gazed out through the trees with such a tense concentration that it really impressed the others. They fell silent.

'Fatty! What are you thinking about?' asked Bets timidly at last. He turned and looked at them all.

'It's Pip's joke,' he said. 'Gosh – to think I never guessed how the thief did it! Pip's solved the mystery!'

The others gaped in surprise.

'How do you mean?' asked Larry at last.

'Can't you see even *now*?' said Fatty impatiently. 'What did Pip do to make us think he was a large-footed thief? He took off his small shoes and put on big ones – and simply danced about over that bed in them. But he's no more got big feet than Bets here! Yet we all fell for his trick.'

'I'm beginning to see,' said Pip.

'And we fell for the thief's trick, which was exactly the same!' said Fatty. He smacked himself hard on the knee. 'We're idiots! We're too feeble for words! We've been looking for a big-footed fellow, and the real thief has been laughing at us all the time – a fellow with small feet – and small hands too!'

'Oh – do you mean he wore big gloves over his hands?' asked Bets. 'To make people think he had both big hands *and* big feet?'

'Of course. He probably wore somebody's big old gardening gloves,' said Fatty. 'And no wonder he left so many clear marks – he *meant* to! He didn't *want* to be careful! The more prints the merrier, as far as he was concerned.'

Light was beginning to dawn very clearly

in everyone's mind now. All that hunting for large-footed, burly, big-handed men! They should have looked for just the opposite.

But who *was* the thief? They knew now he wasn't big – but that didn't tell them the name of the robber.

'I suppose that deep cough was put on too,' said Larry. 'What about those scraps of paper, Fatty? Do they really belong to the mystery?'

'I think so,' said Fatty frowning. 'I'm beginning to piece things together now. I'm . . . *gosh*!'

'What?' said everybody together.

'I think I know who it is!' said Fatty, going scarlet with excitement.

'Who?' yelled everyone.

'Well – I won't say yet in case I'm wrong,' said Fatty. 'I'll have to think a bit more – work things out. But I think I've got it! I think so!'

It was most exasperating that Fatty wouldn't say any more. The others stared at him, trying to read his thoughts.

'If I'm right,' said Fatty, 'all our clues, including the scraps of paper, belong to the mystery – yes, even that roundish print with the criss-cross marks.

And I believe I know how it was that the thief was able to take those big boots about without anyone ever seeing them – and remove the stolen goods too, without anyone ever guessing. Golly, he's clever.'

'Who *is* it?' asked Bets, banging Fatty on the shoulder in excitement.

'Look – I want to go and think this out properly,' said Fatty getting up. 'It's important I should be sure of every detail – very important. I'll tell you for certain this afternoon. Meet here at half past two.'

And with that, Fatty disappeared into the shed with Buster and shut the door! The rest of the company looked at each other in irritation. Blow Fatty! Now they would have to puzzle and wonder for hours!

Fatty opened the door and stuck out his head for one moment. 'If I can think of everything, so can you. You know just as much as I do! Use your brains too, and see what you can make of it all!'

'I can't make *any*thing,' said Pip kicking at the grass. 'The only thing I'm pleased about is that my trick set old Fatty on the right track. I think he's right, don't you? About the thief wearing boots too big for him?'

'Yes. I think he is,' said Daisy, and everyone agreed. She got up. 'Well, come on – Fatty doesn't want us mooning round if he's really going to solve everything and have it all cut and dried. My word – I do hope he thinks it all out before Mr Goon does.'

They all thought hard during the hours that followed. Fatty thought the hardest of all. Bit by bit, he pieced it all together. Bit by bit, things became clear. Of course! All those odd clues did fit together, did make a picture of the thief – and it could only be one thief, nobody else.

Fatty did a spot of telephoning early that afternoon. He telephoned Inspector Jenks and asked him if he could possibly come along at half past two that afternoon. The Inspector was interested.

'Does this by any chance mean that you have solved the latest mystery – the mystery of the big-footed thief?' he asked.

'I hope so, sir,' said Fatty modestly. 'May I ask Mr Goon to come along too, sir? He'll be – er – quite interested too.'

The Inspector laughed. 'Yes, of course. Right,

half past two, and I'll be there at your house.'

Mr Goon was also invited. He was astonished and not at all pleased. But when he heard that the Inspector was going to be present, there was nothing for it but to say yes, he'd be there too. Poor Goon – how he worried and puzzled all the rest of the morning. Did it mean that that big boy had got ahead of him again?

At half past two, the Inspector arrived. Mrs Trotteville was out, as Fatty very well knew. Then Mr Goon arrived. Then the rest of the Find-Outers came, amazed to see Inspector Jenks and Mr Goon sitting in the little study with Fatty.

'Why this room?' asked Bets. 'You never use it for visitors. Is it something to do with the mystery, Fatty?'

'Not really,' said Fatty, who was looking excited and calm all at once. Mr Goon fidgeted, and the Inspector looked at Fatty with interest. That boy! What wouldn't he give to have him as a right-hand man when he was grown-up! But that wouldn't be for years.

'We're all here,' said Fatty, who had got Buster under his chair so that he wouldn't caper round

Mr Goon. 'So I'll begin. I may as well say at once that I've found out who the thief is.'

Mr Goon said something under his breath that sounded like 'Gah!' Nobody took any notice. Fatty went on.

'We had a few clues to work on – very large footprints that were always remarkably well-displayed – and very large gloveprints, also well-displayed so that nobody could possibly miss them. We also had two scraps of paper with "2 Frinton" on one and "1 Rods" on the other. We also had a curious roundish mark on the ground, and that was about all.

'Now – the thing was – nobody ever saw this thief coming or going, apparently, and yet he must have been about for everyone to see – and he apparently had the biggest feet in Peterswood, with the exception of Mr Goon here and Colonel Cross.'

Poor Mr Goon tried to hide his feet under his chair, but couldn't quite manage it.

'Well, we examined every single clue,' said Fatty. 'We followed up the hints on the scraps of paper and went to Frinton Lea. We went to houses and families whose names began with Rod. We visited the cobbler for information about big shoes and he told us about Colonel Cross. Both Mr Goon and I went to see the Colonel – not together, of course – I was doing a spot of weeding, I think, Mr Goon, when you arrived, wasn't I?'

Goon glared but said nothing.

'Well, it was Colonel Cross who put us on the track of where the thief might have got his big boots,' went on Fatty. 'He gives his old ones to jumble sales! And we learnt that he had given a pair to Miss Kay last year for the jumble sale. We guessed that if we could find out who bought them, we'd know the thief!'

Goon made a curious noise and turned it into a throat-clearing.

'We had a shock then, though,' said Fatty. 'The boots hadn't been sold to anyone, they had been stolen! By the thief, of course, for future use! But that brought us to a dead-end. No boots, no thief. We gave up!'

'And then Pip played a trick and showed you how the thief did it!' called out Bets, unable to contain herself. Fatty smiled at her.

'Yes. Pip's trick made me realise that the thief was playing *us* a trick too – the same as Pip's trick! He was wearing very large boots over his small shoes in order to make enormous prints that would make us think he was a big fellow – and the same with his gloves.'

'Ha!' said the Inspector. 'Smart work, Frederick. Very smart!'

'So then I had to change my ideas and begin thinking of a *small* fellow instead of a very big one!' said Fatty. 'One who came unquestioned to our houses, whom nobody would suspect or bother about.'

Mr Goon leaned forward, breathing heavily. The others fixed their eyes on Fatty in excitement. *Now* he was going to tell them the name of the thief!

But he didn't. He paused, as if he were listening for something. They all listened too. They heard the click of a gate and footsteps coming along the path that led along the study wall to the kitchen.

'If you don't mind, sir, I'll introduce you to the thief himself,' said Fatty, and he got up. He went to the door that led from the study into the garden and opened it as a small figure came by.

'Good afternoon,' he said. 'Will you come in here for a minute? You're wanted.'

And in came a small, strutting figure with a basket on his arm – little Twit the baker!

23. WELL DONE, FATTY!

'Twit!' said Mr Goon, and half rose from his chair in amazement. The Inspector looked on, unmoving. All the children gaped, except Fatty, of course. Buster flew out at Twit barking.

'Down, Buster. Back under my chair,' ordered Fatty, and Buster subsided.

Twit looked round in surprise and alarm. 'Here! What's all this?' he said. 'I got my work to do.'

'Sit down,' said the Inspector. 'We want you here for a few minutes.'

'What for?' blustered Twit. 'Here, Mr Goon, what's all this about?'

But Goon didn't know. He sat stolidly and said nothing. He wasn't going to get himself into any trouble by appearing to be friendly with Twit!

'Twit,' said Fatty, 'I've got you in here for reasons of my own. Put your basket down – that's right. Take off the cloth.'

Twit sullenly took off the cloth. Loaves of bread were piled in the basket. Another cloth lay beneath them.

'Take out the loaves and put them on the table,' said Fatty. 'And the cloth under them too.'

'Now what's all this?' said Twit again, looking scared. 'I got my work to do, I tell you. I'm not messing about with my loaves.'

'Do as you're told, Twit,' said the Inspector.

Twit immediately took out his loaves and laid them on the table. Then he took out the cloth beneath them. Fatty looked into the bottom of the basket. He silently took out four things that lay closely packed there – two large boots and two large gloves!

He set them on the table. Twit collapsed on a chair and began to tremble.

'This is how he managed to go about, carrying the boots and gloves, ready for any chance he might have for a little robbery!' said Fatty. 'He never knew what afternoon he might find an easy chance – perhaps nobody in the house except a sleepy maid or mistress – which, as we know, he did find.'

Fatty picked up one of the boots and turned it over. He showed the Inspector the rubber heel. 'I expect, sir, you took a drawing of the footprint on the beds at Norton House,' he said, 'or Mr Tonks did – and so you will see that the rubber heels on these boots and in your drawing are the same. That's proof that the thief wore these boots that Twit has in his basket.'

Fatty turned to the trembling Twit. 'Will you give me your notebook – the one you put down any orders or telephone calls in?' he said. Twit scowled, but put his hand into his pocket and brought out a little pad of cheap paper.

Fatty took it. Then he spoke to Goon. 'Have you got those two scraps of paper on you, Mr Goon?'

Mr Goon had. He produced them. Fatty compared them, and the warning note too, with the paper on the pad. The paper was exactly the same – cheap, thin, and with a fluffy surface.

'Those two scraps of paper you found at Norton House, sir, were bits that Twit had made notes on to remind him of the amount of bread to leave – two loaves for Frinton Lea, and one loaf for Rodways. He apparently makes notes of his orders, and slips them into his basket to remind him. The wind must have blown them out in the garden at Norton House.'

'Gah!' breathed Goon again, staring at the pad of paper and the notes. 'I never thought of that – orders for loaves!'

'Nor did I,' confessed Fatty. 'Not until I began to piece all the clues together properly and found that they added up to the same person – Twit here!'

'Wait a minute,' said Larry. 'How do you explain the thing that puzzled us so tremendously in the Norton House robbery – how did the thief – Twit, that is – come downstairs without being seen by Jinny.'

'That was easy,' said Fatty. 'He simply squeezed himself out of that little window in the boxroom, and slid down the pipe to the ground. He's small enough to do that without much difficulty.'

'Yes – but wait, Fatty – that window was *shut* when I and Tonks went round the house,' said the Inspector. 'He couldn't have escaped through there, and shut it and fastened it from the outside – balanced on the pipe!'

'He didn't shut it *then*,' said Fatty with a grin. 'He simply slid down the pipe, ran to where he had thrown the stolen goods, stuffed them in his basket under the cloth, slipped off the big boots that he had put on over his own small ones – and then went as bold as brass to the back door – appearing there as Twit the baker!'

'And when he went upstairs to look for the thief with Jinny, he carefully shut and fastened the little window he had escaped from!' said Larry, suddenly seeing it all. 'Gosh, that was smart. *He* was the thief – and he came indoors after the robbery and pretended to hunt all round for the robber – and we all thought he was so brave!'

'Gah!' said Goon, looking balefully at Twit. 'Think yourself clever, don't you? Stuffing everybody up with lies – making yourself out a hero too – looking for a thief who was standing in your own shoes!'

'He certainly pulled the wool over everyone's eyes,' said Fatty. 'It was a pretty little trick, and needed quite a lot of boldness and quick thinking. It's a pity he doesn't put his brains to better use.'

'Fatty – what about that funny, roundish mark

– the one with criss-cross lines?' asked Bets. 'Was that a clue too?'

'Yes,' said Fatty, with a grin. 'Come out for a minute and I'll show you what made that mark. I could have kicked myself for not thinking of it before!'

They all crowded to the door except Twit who sat nervously picking at his fingernails. Fatty carried the basket to the door. He set it down in a damp part of the path. Then he lifted it up again.

'Look! It's left a mark of its round shape – and little criss-cross basket lines!' cried Daisy. 'Oh, Fatty – how clever you are!'

'Golly – *I* saw that mark outside Rodways Cottage,' suddenly said Pip. 'Larry, don't you remember – when we were in that cottage with the old woman? The baker came, and left his basket outside to go and put the loaves in the pan. And after he had gone, I noticed the mark his basket had left, and it reminded me of something – of course, it was the drawing in Fatty's book!'

'That's it,' said Fatty. 'That mark was always left where a robbery was committed – because Twit had to stand his basket somewhere, and if he stood it on a dusty path or a damp place, the heavy basket always left a mark. That's why we found those roundish marks at each robbery! If we'd guessed what they were, we would soon have been on the track!'

They were now back in the room. Fatty replaced the loaves in the basket, wrapped up in their cloths.

'No wonder Twit was always so particular about putting cloths over his loaves to keep them clean,' he said. 'They were very convenient for hiding whatever else he had there – not only the boots and gloves, but also anything he stole!'

'Quite smart,' said the Inspector. 'Carried the things he needed for his robbery, as well as his loaves, and also had room for stolen goods too – all under an innocent white cloth. Where did you get all these bright ideas from, Twit?'

Twit said nothing, but gazed sullenly at his smartly-polished little boots, with their highly-polished gaiters.

'Where did you get the big boots from, Twit?' asked Fatty. 'Oh, you don't need to bother to answer. Your cousin, Miss Kay, runs the jumble sale, doesn't she? – and she had the boots given to her for it last year – and you saw them and took them. Goodness knows how many times you've carried those boots round in your basket, hoping to find a chance to wear them and play your big-footed trick!'

'I never stole them,' said Twit. 'I paid for them.'

'Yes – you paid a few coins!' said Fatty. 'Just so that everyone would think you were a kind, generous fellow, paying for jumble sale boots that had been stolen! I heard all about it, and it made me wonder. It didn't seem quite in keeping with what I knew of you.'

Mr Goon cleared his throat. 'I take it you are certain this here fellow is the thief, sir?' he said to the Inspector.

'Well, what do *you* think of the evidence, Goon?' said the Inspector gravely. 'You've been on the job too, haven't you? You must have formed opinions of your own. No doubt you also suspected Twit.'

Mr Goon swallowed once or twice, wondering whether he dared to say yes, he *had* suspected Twit. But he caught Fatty's eye on him, and decided he wouldn't. He was afraid of Fatty and his sharp wits.

'Well, no, sir – I can't say as I suspected the

baker,' he said, 'though I was coming to it. Frederick Trotteville was just one move ahead of me, sir. Bad luck on me! I've tried out all the dodges I learnt at the refresher course, sir – the disguises and all that . . . and . . .'

'Mr Goon! Have you really disguised yourself?' said Fatty, pretending to be amazed. 'I say – you weren't that dirty old tramp, were you? Well, if you were, you took me in properly!'

Goon glared at Fatty. That old tramp! Why, surely it was Fatty himself who had gone shuffling round in tramp's clothes – yes, and eaten his lunch under Mr Goon's very windows. Gah!

'Take Twit away, Goon,' said Inspector Jenks, getting up. 'Arrange with him to find someone to take the bread round, or nobody will have tea this afternoon. Twit, I shall be seeing you later.'

Twit was marched out by Mr Goon, looking very small beside Goon's burly figure. All his strut and cockiness were gone. He was no longer a little bantam of a man, peacocking about jauntily – he looked more like a small, woebegone sparrow.

Inspector Jenks beamed round, and Buster leapt up at him. 'Very nice work, Find-Outers,' he said. 'Very nice indeed. In fact, as my niece Hilary would say – smashing! Now, what about a spot of ice cream somewhere? I'm melting.'

'Oooh yes,' said Bets, hanging on to his arm. 'I knew you'd say that, Inspector! I felt it coming!'

'My word – you'll be as good as Fatty some day, guessing what people think and do!' said the Inspector. 'Well, Frederick, I'm pleased with you – pleased with all of you. And I want to hear the whole story, if you don't mind, from beginning to end.'

So, over double-size ice creams, he heard it with interest and delight.

'It's a curious story, isn't it?' said Fatty, when they had finished. 'The story of a cocky little man who thought the world of himself – and was much too big for his boots!'

Bets gave a laugh and had the last word. 'Yes! So he had to get size twelve and wear those, Fatty – but they gave him away in the end.'

'They did,' said Fatty. 'Well, that's another mystery solved – and here's to the next one! May it be the most difficult of all!'

Look out for the next exciting book in the series...

The Mystery of the Vanished Prince

There is a royal visitor to Peterswood – Prince
Bongawah of Tetarua is staying at a school camp
near the village! But right after he arrives,
he vanishes without a trace. This time the
Find-Outers will have to work *with* Mr Goon
to find the missing prince …

Look out for the next exciting book in the series…

The Mystery of the Strange Bundle

There's a robbery at Mr Fellows' house, but
nothing has been stolen. And the same night of
the robbery, Mr Fellows was seen throwing
a bundle into the river. It's the strangest
mystery yet for the Find-Outers …